The Uncharted Flight

Nirmala Arya

Invincible Publishers

First published in India in 2018

ISBN: 978-93-87328-53-2

This is purely a work of fiction. All characters and episodes described in this book are the product of the author's imagination. Any resemblance to any person, place or incident, living or dead, is entirely coincidental.

Invincible Publishers
G-120, Sushant Lok III, Sector 57, Gurgaon-122002

Registered Address: Opposite Kasturba Ashram, Radaur, Haryana - 135133

Printed at Thomson Press (India) LTD

I dedicate this work to all those hapless ones who have loved and lost someone dear in their lives;
the love lost that chastens you, helps you move on, in time changes into something precious,
becomes an ennobling experience.

Acknowledgement

I remember with gratitude the timely help and encouragement provided by my two daughters, Saritha and Amritha, who helped me with their technical knowledge in typing out the manuscript in the desired format. I must include the similar help extended to me by my son-in-law, Dileep. I am indebted to the editorial team for their help and suggestions, and the various directions in the course of the publication process. I owe a great debt to my late father and my late husband, who had always encouraged my writing. A big thanks to all those famous English novelists and poets, those writers, whose books have always inspired me.

Chapter 1

Random Memories and Vacations

Delving deep into the abyss of her memories, Shalini's mind came up with half remembered images from her childhood, the times she spent her summer vacations at her ancestral house, her paternal home in a remote corner of Northern Kerala, and at a little known village in central Kerala too, where her mother's relatives resided. She used to love those summer months spent with her cousins and uncles and aunts, along with her own family, be it her maternal uncles in central Kerala, or with her father's people at the huge *tharavad* (main house) in a remote corner of North Malabar. Her memory focussed to when she was around eight years old and had gone to her mother's place in central Kerala for her summer vacations.

There was a river about a kilometre away from the main house, where she used to go with her cousins. There were small boats known as '*Vanchis*' tied to posts near the river. Since her uncles were the landlords of the place, they owned many such small boats there. The older boys amongst her cousins knew how to row these boats. They offered to take the younger ones boating. Shalini was excited, despite being a wee bit afraid of venturing out with them. Yet, she overcame her fear and went with one of her cousins. She headed out, when none of the other girls her age were willing to.

Her cousin started rowing the boat. They were only about halfway through the river when the boat flipped over. Luckily for Shalini, the waters were shallow. She had also learnt swimming while at her father's ancestral house which had a huge pond. She was able to swim back to the shore. All the other cousins had a huge laugh at her expense. Her cousin, who had tried to show his rowing skills by taking her with him, emerged from the water totally drenched and looking quite sheepish. He told her that he was sorry for what had happened and offered to take her around once more, promising to be careful this time. But Shalini had second thoughts about accompanying him and abandoned her wish for boating anymore. She ran back to the main courtyard with her other cousins who did not know how to swim.

They used to play a lot of games together, mainly hide and seek, as there were so many places to hide. She thoroughly enjoyed these rough games. She was adventurous in her pursuits, preferring to play boisterous games with her cousins. Thus, most of her vacation was spent at her mother's house along with her maternal cousins.

The other part of her vacation was spent at her father's ancestral house. Certain years had been quite exciting for her there. She tried to conjure up and focus on the confusing images from her childhood years that she had spent at her father's ancestral house.

Deep down the dark passages of her memory, blurry images took shape. They appeared first as dancing images, swaying and swirling around rhythmically. She remembered the rhythmic beat of drums in the background, and a strange music in a local dialect that accompanied those dancing figures. The drumbeats sped up and rose to a crescendo along with the music. The impressionable eight year old that Shalini was, watched in fear and wonder, perched on her uncle's lap. The huge formidable shapes that gathered around in a semi-circle had struck a chill in her. Later, her uncle, her father's elder brother, explained to her that the thing she had witnessed was a form of a masked tribal dance, known as a '*theyyam*', which was both religious and ritualistic. It was associated with the superstitious beliefs of the people of the surrounding villages, including the inmates of her father's ancestral house.

She distinctly remembered the main performer – they were called the special actors, or the '*theyyams*' of North Malabar – the one who was called '*Theechamundi*' who jumped repeatedly into a bonfire helped by his aides. This form of theatrical, religious and ritualistic dance was performed once every four years at her father's ancestral house called by the name '*Malayarattu*'. The ritualistic perambulations, along with the prayers uttered loudly in the local dialect by the performer, were supposed to ward off evil spirits in and around the *tharavad* (the main house). It was sponsored by different members of the family for the wellbeing of those residing within the family. There were other '*theyyams*' of lesser importance too, but they were only meant for providing entertainment to the viewers. The very getup of these '*theyyams*' – with their huge coloured headgear – was a visual treat to the onlookers, as each actor wore a unique gear and brightly painted wooden face masks, with a predominance of red colour on them. Their dresses were made out of green coconut palm fronds waist down, which seemed to swell and contract with each forward and backward movement of the performer.

The eight-year-old Shalini could not take her eyes off of the brightly coloured, black, red and green costumes of the *theyyams*, with their huge headgear, also coloured in imposing white, red and black, interspersed with green. These actions of the '*theechamundi*' (where the actor jumps into the flaming pyre of logs) really frightened her, but held her enthralled. She wondered whether the actor would himself get consumed in flames. How was she to know that the person enacting that particular character was in fact a seasoned performer? They had taken enough precautions not to get burnt by the leaping flames of the bonfire. These *'attams'*, as the dance rituals were commonly called, were also a part of the yearly temple festivities of that locality, usually performed by a particular group of people called the *'Malayans'*, she learnt later. Shalini was thus initiated into the world of traditional folk performing arts at an early age.

Her fascination with the traditional art forms of Kerala, especially that of *theyyams* and later the *Kathakali,* increased as she literally grew up amidst these local art enthusiasts, including her many uncles, who regularly sponsored those events. The performing artists of *Theyyams* were the *'Vannans'* or *'Malayans'* who traditionally belonged to a different caste. Traditionally, they were the people belonging to a lower social strata in an ordinary sense, but when they performed the religious and ritualistic dances, they were considered akin to Gods. They came in their *theyyam* attires and after giving a sterling performance, they blessed the people around, including their sponsors. All this was explained much later to Shalini by her father and her own uncle.

During her vacations, she loved to go to the countryside where her father's ancestral home was situated. It was a beautiful and pristine place with hills shielding a distant horizon, a winding river, dense forests and mangroves near the sprawling house, temples and ponds, and acres of paddy fields. Shalini had hordes of cousins there too. She loved to roam about with her cousins, pluck raw green mangoes during its season, and relish them with a bit of salt, coconut oil and red chillies that practically melted in their mouths. This delicious experience was beyond words for her. They loved to swim for hours in the pond near their main house till noon and then reach home all exhausted and hungry, ready to gorge themselves on a fulfilling meal. There was a kitchen outside the main house, used mainly to cook meals for the labourers in the fields.

Exhausted after their games, Shalini and her cousins used to visit the outer kitchen somedays, partaking themselves stealthily of the appetizing healthy lunch prepared for the labourers, which was usually rice gruel with '*chakkapuzhukku*' - a tasty dish made with jackfruit, on which she and her cousins would feast themselves. It tasted far better to them than the rich spread of various different dishes that they were given within the house. All this was done without the knowledge of the elders of the house, who would have blown their top off, had they come to know of this. She often found herself fascinated by the way the labourers, after a hard day in the fields, ate huge mounds of rice out of a crude plate made from plantain leaves placed upon a square frame, again made out of the soft inner bark of a banana tree. She observed that a few huge scoops of either rice or rice gruel was served to each person, along with some curry and pickle that had been prepared beforehand. The way the labourers fell upon their food hungrily, and filled themselves up with fat portions of food that disappeared down their throats, amazed Shalini and her cousins who tried it out themselves after a tiring day of play. It was definitely the sheer relish of the taste, their well-deserved wage for a day of toil in the fields, which made their simple fare so appetising to them. As for Shalini and her cousins themselves, she found that such secretive meals after a good swim were far more delicious and satisfying than the regular meals provided to them inside the main house.

Then there were the games they played within the house, in the huge and expansive attic on the third floor which was not frequented often by the critical elders. They used to clear some space amidst the rubble and dumped items there. They even had a small fire pit there. They used to steal food items from the store near the main kitchen and play at 'keeping house', with the oldest amongst them playing the father and the mother, which the rest of them became their children. There would be a spate of imitations with her cousins who were good at it, taking on the roles of the family elders. There were times when the youngsters were bold enough to perform actual plays, episodes from the epic Mahabharata. They would often take the moving stories of mythical heroes, like Dhruv or Prahlad. They were profusely encouraged in this by all the family members, even by the elders, and were made to perform on a temporary stage put up at one end of the long balcony over the main courtyard. Shalini loved the thrill of those days, the discovery of a wee bit of dramatic talent within herself as she took on the roles of Dhruv's mother, or that of Draupadi in the scenes enacted from the '*Kalyanasougandhikam*' episode. These incidents were interspersed with actual Kathakali performances made by the local troupe during special festive occasions. The performances which she enjoyed the most were the ones that went on for the entire duration of the night.

Shalini loved to lose herself in the nostalgic memories of those days; she treasured them and carried them around in her mind for years that came after. She became assertive and bold in her formative years due to the comparative freedom she had enjoyed along with her male cousins when she had been young. She was unaware of the restrictions that were imposed over her not-so-fortunate female cousins. This was also because her father, being more educated and broadminded than her traditional uncles, gave her more freedom in her actions. Of course as she grew older and received more education and exposure, she became more conscious of the societal restrictions within her Kerala Brahmin community. Back home, she was careful not to overstep her so called 'limitations'. These thoughts definitely influenced her actions, as she found herself not too comfortable those days in mingling with people who were below her social rank. However, she could not control her interest in the opposite sex, which made her observant of youngsters, especially the young presentable males, around her. She noticed the friends of her cousins, who frequented their company. This was how she started observing Chandran, a smart student of Kathakali and also a member of the troupe which was sponsored by her paternal uncles. She was yet unaware of the tremendous impact that a meeting with him would produce in her life, and the far reaching effect it would go on to have on her.

Chapter 2

The Lure of Kathakali and More

Her mother was the only sister amongst her siblings, so her uncles indulged and spoilt her and her family whenever they visited them. On festive and other special occasions, they often arranged a Kathakali performance for the sake of the visiting relatives. These maternal uncles owned a Kathakali troupe themselves and made arrangements to give training to the performers too, which made it easy for them to arrange for all night performances of Kathakali. Shalini was introduced to the nuances of Kathakali as an art form by her uncles and her mother. They were the real connoisseurs of the art form. One or two of Shalini's cousins were actually learning Kathakali themselves. She loved watching them learn. An *acharya* used to come to the house to teach them. Shalini's love of the incomparable art form of Kerala, Kathakali, had thus begun at an early age. Being interested in music, she loved listening to the beats that went with the performance of Kathakali, on a percussion instrument called the '*chenda*', which is a compulsory accompaniment to the enactment of a Kathakali drama. Her mother had initiated her into the differences between the performances given at her place and those performed at her husband's home.

Both Shalini and her mother were avid observers of these performance styles. She was lucky that her father's cousins managed a local Kathakali troupe along with a *'Kalari'*, a martial arts training centre, which served as a training ground for the artists. They gave performances during special events, sponsored by her paternal uncles. The northern style and the southern style of enacting the Kathakali dance drama thus became familiar to her. Her mother was all praises for the acting styles of the Kathakali artists at her own place. Shalini appreciated both the styles, recognising and appreciating the uniqueness of each style of performance.

When she had been younger, she was unable to understand the intricate details of the dance drama. Instead, she was just impressed by the colourful nature of their attire and the majestic performances. But as she grew older, her mother's expert guidance enabled her to appreciate their subtle actions and muted speech, denoted by *'mudras,'* the symbolic mode of communication of the Kathakali artists on stage. She also learned about the music in the background, the *'kathakali padam'*, set to haunting, yet soulful melodies, accompanied by a rhythmic beat which was generated with a plate like structure struck at regular intervals by a hard stick. This was called *'elathalam'*, which lent an added attraction to the Kathakali music. When watching a Kathakali performance, one could mentally enter into the play at any point, as the general audience was familiar with the stories being enacted from popular Indian epics. This did not detract from the total magical effect of a Kathakali performance at all. Shalini understood this well by watching the enacted plays which completely bewitched her. Their influence stayed with her all her life.

During a vacation at her father's place when she was about fourteen years old, she was introduced for the first time to the main actors backstage. She was specially observant of one person there. He was the lead actor in many of the plays that they had enacted, especially those in the stories from the Mahabharata. He came on stage as Krishna, as Nala, as Arjuna and other such virtuous heroes and demonstrated his expertise in doing the *'Pacha – vesham'* (actors donning the characters of noble persons). His performance captivated her. His name was Chandran, short for Chandrasekharan Nair. His physical stature was perfectly suited for the rigorous training of a Kathakali artist. As kids, they were allowed to go and watch them train their bodies to mould into the required shape that suited their art. Even at that time, she had noticed Chandran with his perfectly chiselled body. His oiled chest muscles, narrow waist and abs, toned arms and legs stood out as he exercised, granting him a strange glow, made even more mysterious by the intense piercing nature of his grey eyes. He was blessed with sharp features, though his complexion was on the darker side. She had felt drawn by the aura of his intensity and physical fitness. She secretly admired him, and waited to catch a glimpse of him outdoors.

Then came the day of an all-night Kathakali performance during a festive occasion. With bated breath, she had watched the episode of *'Doothu'* by Sri Krishna; when Krishna goes to the Kauravas' court as a peace maker, begging them to give the Pandavas at least a portion of their land. The Kauravas refuse to part with even a bit of their land. Enraged at Krishna, they bind him in retaliation. Krishna then shows them his *'Viswaroopam'*, which bewilders them into a temporary submission. That was the story of the play which Shalini watched with rapt attention. She was mesmerised with the outstanding performance of her favourite actor Chandran in the role of Krishna. During the act, she noticed a hypnotizing, probing quality of his eyes that look out towards the audience and made his actions even more vivid. She came to admire all the mythological characters he represented on stage, especially that of Sri Krishna.

She started noticing him more frequently offstage too; on her way to the temple nearby, when she passed by his house near the paddy field, when she was roaming around with her cousins. Earlier, she never noticed him among the group of youngsters that she used to meet during her walks, but after her uncles introduced her to the troupe members during their practise sessions at the backroom of their courtyard at the *Kalary*, she was able to observe him better, and at close quarters. The contours of his body were perfect, his glowing complexion had been toned by regular exercise and practise of *Kalary*. His skin shone during the training, due to some oil that seemed to have been applied all over. A well maintained and toned physique, with rippling muscles shining in all their sensuous glory, really appealed to her. She hastily averted her eyes when she realized that he had been observing her with his intense probing eyes too. He stood out amongst all the other players. He seemed well mannered and respectful towards the elders of her family, who in-turn encouraged him well. Thus, it happened so that she witnessed him practising multiple times those days. He was no more than a few years older than her. She carried the crush that she had developed for him into her adolescence. As she grew up, she got restricted from venturing out of the women's interior courtyard alone. Sighting the player then became a rare opportunity, which she eagerly looked forward to. Over the passage of time, her feelings for him got buried deep inside her heart and mind that dared not surface for the fear of social stigma. She was in awe of the elders of the family and their unwritten laws regarding the behaviour of women within the family.

Once when she was about sixteen years of age, she was at at her father's place and was engaged in reading a book, seated within the interiors of the house. The women folk were not allowed to be seen outside the courtyard, which was frequented by the men of the household. She was on the thresh hold of sweet sixteen at that time, her heart filled with yearnings unfamiliar to her. She had also started to feel shy in appearing with her grown up male cousins, or play any more games with them. She rather preferred to move about with the other girls her age, or to curl up with a book alone, as she was engaged in at that moment. She was seated by a window which opened out to the outer courtyard. She suddenly noticed her senior uncle talking to some person there. On a closer observation, she recognised this person as the artist and her childhood crush, Chandran. She peered more closely. He stood at a respectful distance from her uncle and was responding calmly to her uncle's queries. They were discussing his future prospects. Her uncles were ready to sponsor the remaining of his education at *Kalamandalam,* the best institute for Kathakali in Kerala, as he had proved himself to be the best trainee in their house troupe. He seemed to be overwhelmed at their generosity. As he stood by with gratitude, her eyes suddenly got locked with his. An electrifying pulse passed between them. She gazed upon him in the entirety of his physical prowess. He must also have found this unexpected sight of her from inside the building to have shaken him a bit. He withdrew his gaze in silent haste the very next instant. Perhaps, he felt that it was highly improper to look upon a lady of the big house that way, though he did feel a certain attraction towards her. The thought made him fear losing out on the excellent opportunity of his future education, which depended entirely on being in the good books of his benefactors. He knew he belonged to a lower caste and class of his society, and that it was not permissible or possible for him to go beyond the limits set for people like him by the society of their times. Shalini did not seem, at that moment, to have any such hang ups. She gave herself up to enjoying the intense piercing gaze of the man. At that moment, she imagined the look in his eyes to be that of Sri Krishna, the flute player, on stage. Her heated imagination, fed on a diet of romantic novels, conjured up an image of the God of Love, amidst the *gopis* of Vrindavan, the endearing flute player that Chandran had portrayed so many times on stage. She longed to be one among those *gopis*. But the very next instant, everything had come crashing down. He had averted his gaze and was moving away from her vantage point. Though she had considered meeting him outside, she knew that it was a task that was next to impossible. She gave up all hope of it.

As for Chandran, it had come to him as a shocker at that vulnerable instant. His future was being decided by the elders of the *tharavad*. He had never expected to be confronted so suddenly with such an intense look from the girl of his dreams. That indeed she was, as he had developed a burning attraction for her ever since he had glimpsed her both amidst the audience during his performance and outside during his training. He worshipped the very ground she treaded on. On a sudden impulse, he had met her powerful gaze. After meeting her gaze unexpectedly and holding it for an instant, he had diverted his eyes forcefully. Inherently cautious, he could not take the risk of the elders noticing it. This action had been extremely painful for him, but inevitably necessary. He had wanted to take proper leave of this charming girl, to tell her about his future being decided, but that was not to be. He couldn't dare to speak with her, considering the watchful eyes of traditionalists all around the place. He was packed off, bag and baggage, the same evening to an institution where he was to complete all his future studies. He knew that the embers of the spark that had been ignited that day, were to be buried deep down within his psyche. They could never burst into flames of desire, however much he wanted them to. She was unattainable.

She belonged to the most powerful patriarchal Brahmin family of their locality. A meeting with one much below her social position, as Chandran was a Nair, would not only have been frowned upon in those days, but also vehemently objected and opposed to. Her mother made sure that she was always chaperoned, with either a relative or a servant. A blossoming romance, she felt, was thus nipped in the bud. That was the last time she ever saw him at that ancient homestead, amidst the conventional set up of her paternal house. Memories of these incidents receded to the backyard of her mind over time. He got taken up with busier things in life as well.

Chapter 3
The Off-Campus Adventure

After this episode, Shalini soon returned to her hometown with her parents, where her father had been settled with his job. Her visits to the native places became few and far between. She was taken up with her studies too. She studied classical dance and South Indian classical music on her mother's insistence. She gradually started appreciating and enjoying these performing arts too, but her father always insisted that she pursue her studies instead. He was prepared to let her study upto the post-grad level and even beyond if she so desired. Both her father and she waved off her mother's wish that she should get married and settle down after her PG. She wanted to pursue higher studies first and get settled with a job. Her academically oriented father fully supported her in this.

Thus, it was by the strength of an academic grant that after completing her PG, she was able to join a PhD course at Delhi University. Her only brother who was younger to her, got admission at an engineering institute near their parents' house. So, when she left for Delhi, she was relieved that her brother would be close to their parents till he landed a job at least, as was the expected custom in those days.

The Delhi University campus was a different world altogether for her. There were so many aspirants there for higher studies from different parts of the world, and not just

India. She was thus introduced to a cosmopolitan culture there. Her college life back home had been singularly uneventful, except for an occasional appearance on stage as a light music performer, for which she had been awarded a prize and had been congratulated amply. When younger, Shalini had not been too conscious of her looks, but in college she came to realize her share of admirers. Her fair, supple and beautifully toned figure, her flawless wheatish complexion and aquiline features, coupled with her intelligence, won her some rave comments. Boys her age were in awe of her. They did not dare to flirt with her, although she never hesitated to join in all their fun. She could not find a boy who was mature enough to share her thoughts and inclinations. Many of her friends, on understanding her nature, left her alone to pursue her own interests. She did not have time to pursue her interests in music and dance, due to her academic commitments.

An inborn restraint that a conventional upbringing had ingrained in her made her avoid late night parties hosted by her friends. Though she was aware of the modern trends in partying, she preferred to avoid them and spend time by herself. She used to go for long walks with similar minded friends, both inside as well as outside her campus. These walks were invigorating for her, both physically and mentally. Sometimes, after her research work, she preferred to go for walks alone. She also liked to visit the historical monuments of Old Delhi when time permitted, and also the museums of art. She loved visiting them more than going on shopping sprees with her female friends at the shopping malls in New Delhi. A nostalgia for her own past, filled with memories of her time spent at her paternal and maternal houses, overflowed her mind during such moments.

It was during one of her strolls outside the campus on the western side, that she decided to pass through a hitherto unfamiliar side street. Almost a year had passed since she had come to Delhi University. After walking for a few minutes, she chanced upon a huge building on the right side of the road, with a big poster put up across the front. It read, 'Delhi Institute of Kathakali,' Proprietor and Director, one Mr. Chandrasekharan Nair. She wondered in surprise whether it could be the same Chandran whom she had known during her younger days. *But here, in Delhi?* Overcome with curiosity, she decided to find out.

She entered the building. She stepped into a foyer from which there were entrances to different parts of the building, which consisted of three floors. On enquiry, she was directed to the director's room. When Shalini stepped into the plush interiors of the office, she found it slightly dark compared to the outside. It was an air-conditioned room, beautifully furnished. Her eyes took a little time to adjust. She could make out the director seated on a comfortable seat at the farthest end facing the door. On seeing her enter, the man in a deep blue suit rose up politely and addressed her, "Yes, madam, how can I be of service to you?" The query was in perfect English, with just a trace of an accent. "Madam, please take a seat." She hurriedly took the seat that was offered to her. He sat down in his own chair after she had taken a seat.

"Have you come to book a Kathakali performance? Would you prefer the play *'Nala-Charitham'*, or *'Kuchela Vritham'*? Which club do you represent? Do you want the show to last for a few hours show or perhaps an all-night performance?" His words flowed out with the ease of a practised professional.

There was little or no resemblance between this man and the Chandran that she remembered. But the clean-shaven look, the strong jaws and the eyes, and the piercing quality of his intense grey eyes betrayed the former artist. She recognized him the instant he smiled and turned his gaze upon her. Did he not wonder why a poised good-looking young lady had entered his office so long after office hours? Did he really imagine that she had come to book a play?

She found herself momentarily confused at his barrage of questions. She then replied haltingly, "Mr Chandran, I have not come here to book a Kathakali show. I have come here just to meet you."

He was taken aback for an instant. Gathering his wits, he asked with a surprised look, "Who are you? Why did you come at this time?" He was peering at her closely now. This beautiful and smart young woman had come looking for him. *Why*, he wondered. A growing concern showed on his face. He ransacked his memory. She did look familiar to him, but he could not place her. She looked so modern, stylish, and intellectual.

"Mr. Chandran, don't you remember me? Long ago, you were an upcoming Kathakali student at my father's place, the big *tharavad* back in Kerala and I was a young girl back then, remember? At the big house? Are you not the same Chandransekharan Nair who used to perform at the ancestral house in a remote village of North Kerala? I used to come and watch your performances as a young girl. I belonged to the big house."

Chandran sprang up at the shock of remembrance. "Oh! You are the *Kochuthamburatti*!" That was how the servants and other dependents used to address her.

"How come you are here? After so many years? Well, I never imagined I'd ever get to meet you again, and here in Delhi, of all places."

To put him at ease, Shalini replied, "You see, I have come here for my higher studies. After completing my PG back home, I came here to pursue a PhD. I am staying at the university campus."

Chandran could not sit in front of her anymore. Age old conditioning of the by–gone eras, the complex of caste differences seemed to come back to haunt him, making him don a subservient posture in front of her. Shalini insisted that he take a seat, threatening to walk out if he did not comply.

"See, Mr. Chandran. There is no need for this kind of a formal behaviour. We are miles away from home. Forget the nonsense that was practised earlier. Here we are just individuals equal to each other. Do act practically."

Chandran sat down, though with an uneasy expression. Shalini was comforted. Now they could observe each other better, after the initial shock of recognition. Even after a gap of almost seven years, he looked the same, she began to realize. His well-built physique, his thick curly hair with a high forehead, his sharp clean-shaven features were all exactly as she remembered. His olive dark skin seemed to have lightened a bit, perhaps due to the Delhi temperature. She remembered him in a traditional Kerala style dhoti and banian; thus the suit seemed a bit out of place, though it was well tailored and fitted very well over his body. When he held out his hand, she noticed that his long artistic fingers were just the same as she remembered them. His intense, probing grey eyes, with a mysterious smouldering depth in them, seemed to draw her towards him once again.

Chandran, on his part, could not believe his eyes. This apparition, whom he had secretly admired, when he had caught glimpses of her on her way to the temple or in the premises of the big house, was actually standing before him!

Chandran's memories rushed back in his mind which had kept them suppressed for so long. He remembered how he had observed this perfect maiden whose movements had haunted him, and the stolen glances they had shared when he met her on the way to the temple near the big house. She must have noticed him too, the way she had stood with eyes closed, hands folded before the presiding deity. He had stood some distance away, hoping and praying that she would bestow her glance upon him. She had appeared to his heated imagination as a goddess personified. And oh, the thrill that had coursed through his veins when she accidentally chanced to look at him! Those were the only times he could actually see her outside the confines of the big house. That or when she wandered among the mangroves with her cousins. He had never known whether she reciprocated his feelings or not. He had never confronted her directly. Those days and times, people like him, belonging to his caste, could not dare to even think of communicating with such high-born women, even through gestures. Thus, he was very discreet and kept his admiration to himself, satisfying himself with catching such fleeting glimpses of this unattainable maiden.

All this had come to an abrupt end when the elders at the *tharavad,* his benefactors, decided to sponsor all his further studies in Kathakali. He was packed off to a prestigious institution for Kathakali, the Kerala Kalamandalam, as he was a brilliant, earnest and promising young Kathakali student of their local troupe. He still remembered the meeting he had had with the elders, standing outside the main courtyard when his future course was being decided. As they were talking amongst themselves, ignoring his presence nearby, he let his eyes wander beyond the group and towards the windows that opened towards the interiors. He had had the shock of his life when his eyes inadvertently locked with the curious eyes of the very same person he had been unconsciously searching for! For a moment he had wondered whether those eyes held the same yearning and desire that he had felt coursing through his veins? It had been an unguarded moment for both of them. He had quickly averted his eyes to save his future from being at stake, as it would not have augured well with his sponsors had they found out that he was harbouring forbidden thoughts about a girl from their house. Those powerful patrons would have even finished him off in those times. He could not imagine himself as a hero of some film who would dare to carry off his heroine to some charmed territory and lived happily ever after. Too much was at stake – his career, his future, the peaceful existence of his family and her reputation. So, he had surrendered to his fate that was being decided by his sponsors.

Chandran remembered dismissing those unholy thoughts from his mind as soon as they had sprung up. He had not wanted to show a lack of gratitude towards his benefactors. He was merely being practical and cautious; it was his duty to stand up to their expectations. He definitely wanted to be known as a good artist in his chosen field. So, he chose not to pursue his feelings and emotions at that stage. He had left it at that. He believed that she must also have let those mad moments pass into oblivion, if ever she had such hidden thoughts within herself too. He believed it to have been the hot young blood that had coursed through him then, making him harbour such feelings. But his social conditioning was hard to live down. He had always lacked a strong will to assert himself. He obediently took the course directed to him by the respected elders. He left his native place to pursue his career, his secret one-sided affair, as he believed it had been, confined to the recesses of his mind.

Chandran had then applied himself totally to his study of Kathakali and the pursuance of his career. He had completed his basic education to the level of plus two. His diligent efforts made him rise up to the status of the best student at the Kathakali Institute, further to be a better artist and much later, the best instructor. Later, some of his Kathakali fans and sponsors supported him to establish the 'International Arts Institute', which specialized in Kathakali studies at Delhi, of which he was made the Director. Here, he personally supervised the teaching of Kathakali. There were other departments for the propagation of dance studies like Bharatanatyam, Kuchipudi, Odissi, and other folk dances, under the tutelage of famous artists and tutors in those respective fields. Chandran's 'Kathakali Academy' had grown to be the most famous one. This was the institute that Shalini had stumbled upon on one of her jaunts.

However, this present meeting with the same girl, Chandran couldn't bring himself to believe. He was speechless. The woman of his childhood dreams had appeared before him in flesh and blood! The unattainable 'Devi' was right in front of him, asking him to renew their acquaintance. They slipped into an easy, amicable discussion about their careers and lives up to the present. Shalini understood that he had diligently made his way up. He had not married yet, concentrating more on his career, though his folks back home were persuading him to 'settle down'. The Institute he headed was doing pretty well too. Students from all over India and abroad had enrolled in this academy, many of them Kathakali enthusiasts. Chandran had the proud demeanour of a successful *'acharya'* of Kathakali. He was the main instructor of the art at the institute. In his spare time, he tried to learn the Kathakali *sangeet*. Sometimes, he confessed, he dabbled in oil painting, but he was only an amateur in these arts.

On her part, she had nothing much to confess about her personal career. She had taken her studies seriously, had duly completed her PG with flying colours and finally landed a research fellowship that brought her to the portals of Delhi University to pursue a Ph.D. in her choice of topic, she informed him. However, she appreciated all types of artistic pursuits and had studied Carnatic music for some time back home.

Time just flew past. Suddenly, Shalini remembered that she had to return to her hostel. Though as a Ph.D. student, there weren't too many restrictions for her, she was expected to return back at a reasonable time. Deciding to meet at a later date, they exchanged their phone numbers and took leave of each other. Back at her hostel room, Shalini finally got the time to ruminate. It was clear that she had taken Chandran by surprise. She also could not believe her luck. To have come across her childhood dream boy after all these years! The very first person she had fantasised about. Resplendent in his Kathakali gear, he had been to her the very symbol of the lotus-eyed Lord Sri Krishna, back in those days.

Now at present, she was nearer to him than she could have ever imagined being in those days. Here, there was no one to restrain her – no familial or societal *'Lakshman Rekha'* imposed on her, she felt. She felt far removed from the societal restrictions of her family. Were they mentally so far removed in real life, as their society had wanted them to be? She had to disagree. She decided to take up where they had left off, she wanted to get to know him better and decided to do just that.

Perhaps, it would lead to something meaningful in her life, she thought. She hoped that their relationship would turn out to be a lasting one. She knew that she was taking, what she felt was, an 'uncharted flight' in her life. It could lead her to uncharted realms of happiness and excitement if it was on the correct track. But if it crashed midair, it could lead to ruin, a battered and shattered body and mind, for both of them. Whatever the case, she definitely wished to take up the risk, a calculated gamble in her life.

They decided to meet the day after. He rung her up to discuss the time that was convenient for both of them to meet. She approached the venue of their meeting with mixed feelings. She was excited at the thought of getting to know him all over again, but still feared the possibility of him not falling in with her ideas? On reaching, she found him already seated at a table He looked quite presentable and impeccable in his suit. He was not too tall, just two or three inches above her five feet three inches of height. She looked at him transfixed as he got up to draw out a chair for her in a courteous manner. Chandran seemed to be a bit nervous. He couldn't trust himself to act in the most gentlemanly manner, as he usually did in front of other women who came to his office for an admission or a booking. Shalini recognised his hesitation. She wanted to put him at ease.

"Now, Chandran, before we proceed, I would like to make one thing clear. Do not, I repeat, go back to calling me *Kochuthamburatti*. You can please call me Shalini, or Shalu for short, which is what I prefer."

"Oh! How could I?" He knew that it would not come easy. The old habits haunted him and he found it difficult to break off from them. But he dared not risk losing her acquaintance once again. He knew that he was not as indifferent as he wanted to believe, to her offer of a real friendship.

"You have to try. See how I came around to calling you by your name? Just look upon me as a long-lost friend. Come on, let's take a walk. Or let us board a bus to Karol Bagh, if you do not mind being late. I want to buy a few essentials."

Fortunately for Shalini, Chandran was not too busy at the moment. He offered to take his car, but then decided that taking a walk with her was better, to the nearby places at least. There was always the option to take a bus if need be.

They walked for almost an hour and then took the bus and back. It was the most memorable walk in many years for both of them. They grew oblivious to their surroundings. The majesty and grandeur of the city of Delhi was lost on them. They had so much to tell each other, to catch up and share experiences from their past, each unique to either of them, due to the different circumstances that they grew up in. Although, they did have some similarities, mostly in their common appreciation for performative arts and music, mainly Indian light and classical.

He reminded her that he had risen from a middle class background. They were dependent on the local aristocratic landlord, the family which Shalini belonged to, for their livelihood. He was interested to learn the Kathakali as an art form, more than a conventional school learning at that time, though he had acquired some basic education. It was fortunate for him that they had started a private Kathakali troupe, and that he was selected to be a part of the troupe as he had shown great talent in the art form of Kathakali very early on. A local master had initiated him into the basics of the art form. He had gained experience by taking part in the local performances put up for the sake of his sponsors on special occasions. That was how Shalini had chanced upon his sterling performances.

She understood that he had a family back home, comprising of a mother and an aged grandmother. Both his sisters had already been married off well. His father had died and he had since taken up the responsibility of his family. Not one to forget his roots, he maintained constant contact with them and visit his native place whenever required. Settled in Delhi, he seemed to be a man comfortably well off. He regretted having missed conventional education, so he took a degree in his chosen subject of fine arts with a three-year private correspondence course, after completing the basic tenth and plus two levels at home. He had to take his practical sessions as part of the contact program at a nearby education centre. He attended two or three courses in spoken English, which perfected his English-speaking capabilities. This helped him in communicating with the British, American and other foreigners who thronged his classes in order to learn about Kathakali as an art. When time would permit, he planned to do his PG too, he informed Shalini.

She did not have much to recount. She had had a protected childhood. Her studies had gone on unhampered. Whenever they had the time, her family took trips to their native place. They occasionally witnessed Kathakali performances during festive occasions. She had missed Chandran's presence after he left. Her parents were also members of clubs which propagated this art form, back in their hometown Whenever she got some time off from her studies, she accompanied them to attend such art and cultural activities of the club, which almost always included a '*Kathakali Aattam*'. She became familiar with most eminent and famed artists of the time specializing in Kathakali. Yet, she yearned to watch a performance by Chandran, which never happened in those days. Slowly, time wiped out the memories associated with his roles in her mind, even though her enthusiasm for this great traditional art form did not wane one bit.

Chapter 4
Moonlit Romance

During the course of exchange of their shared memories of the countryside back at their native place, they found that they shared a common admiration for the beauty of those far-off places in Kerala. The sights that she most enjoyed were from the train rides through her homeland, from one end to the other during daytime, from her hometown in the south to her native place at the farthest end in the north. She was never tired of watching the sights and scenes from the train window as it sped past the beautiful wild sights on either side. Her mind was enraptured by the sight of the thronging coconut palms with their swaying fronds in the breeze at a distance, which seemed to be beckoning to her. With small thatched huts, fields and cattle roaming nearby, acres of cultivated paddy fields, the bewitching backwaters, the sights of nearby temples and mosques, and the shallow ponds where the *'bhakts'* took occasional dips lifted her spirits. The rice fields gave the impression of an alluring rolled out green carpet, taking on a golden hue at times when bathed in the warm rays of the setting sun. The occasional backwaters lent an air of charm and unalloyed beauty to the atmosphere. Night travel by train shut out all these endearing sights, so Shalini preferred travelling by day. It was just a matter of five or six hours.

Much later, when she had a chance to visit some western countries as part of her educational programme and could see the beautiful landscapes there, she could not help comparing those places to the places back home in Kerala. In those western countries, the sights were extremely good, cool and comforting, but most of it was man-made. The neatness there was wonderful, but she missed the wild beauty of the Kerala landscapes. No wonder, it is called 'God's Own Country'. As far as natural beauty went, there was no place as attractive with as good a tropical climate, she wholeheartedly felt, even when compared to places in the Northern parts of India.

Chandran agreed with all her views regarding nature's bounty in Kerala, their homeland. He had also been on foreign tours with his Kathakali troupe. He had also visited some of the counties abroad and gone for sight-seeing as part of those tours. He had to admit, like Shalini, that he considered his homeland more blessed in natural beauty than the many places he had observed in far-away lands. However, they agreed that the people back there did not realise it or treat the land with due concern, especially in maintaining basic cleanliness. Both of them were partly hit by nostalgia and decided to visit their native place when they could take some time off of their present commitments. For the time being, however they decided to go on local sight–seeing tours in and around Delhi. Shalini was pleased that Chandran was also enthusiastic about travel and touring. Though they had previously been to places in separate groups, they now decided to go together. When both of them were able to take some time off, they decided to visit the Taj Mahal, by moonlight.

Shalini was looking forward to the trip with great anticipation. She was determined to make it a perfect trip. Her romantic fancies had started soaring. Though she had seen the Taj Mahal before, it was in the day-time on one of the guided tours with friends from her university, it was a different experience. She had then had only a pure academic interest, besides the curiosity of a tourist. Even then, she had been overwhelmed by the sheer technical beauty of the construction, though she had felt let down by the cold distancing of the marble building. Perhaps it was because she had witnessed it in the afternoon, with the scorching hot sun beating down mercilessly over the marble floors of the vast building, making them blistering hot. The romantic atmosphere had been absent, though she could imagine the great love between the historical characters of Shah Jahan and Mumtaz Mahal that inspired the construction of the wondrous monument. At that point, however, Shalini had felt let down by the sight of the historical Taj. She had not mentioned it to her friends, who were ecstatic over the sight. She had overheard someone say that the romantic beauty of the Taj comes alive when observed on a moonlit night. She had decided then that if ever she got the chance, she would come back and visit the place by moonlight. She had now finally got the chance, that too with Chandran.

Both of them decided to take this trip on a holiday. They were both free on the Sunday they selected. Chandran had first wanted to take his car, but the prospect of the long drive back through unfamiliar roads was a bit daunting, so they decided to take a local tourist vehicle which was scheduled to bring them to the premises of the Taj by evening. Along the route, they were to visit a few other tourist spots too, places of historical significance on the outskirts of Agra city, Fatehpur Sikri, etc. Shalini wondered why there were so many tombs on their route. It was a depressing thought that infected her current happy frame of mind. It seemed to foreshadow how their feelings were also going to be entombed thus in future, in some remote corner of their minds.

But fortunately, such thoughts did not register consciously on her imagination. All her attention was on Chandran himself, who was busy pointing these places of historic interest to her. He mentioned having brought his students to these places some time back. She was intent on admiring the elegant manner in which he conducted himself, his courteous manners towards other tourists, and his gentle concern for her wellbeing during the journey. She enjoyed sitting close to him in the vehicle. He looked handsome in a well-tailored blue suit, blue seemed to be his favourite colour, as it was hers too. She also enjoyed a good glimpse of the outlines of his perfect frame as she snuggled close. She knew that she looked good in her pretty pale violet silky churidar. Her wavy tresses danced in the breeze as she chatted away about the experiences she had had at the University. Chandran was a patient listener who observed her with avid interest. He seemed to be a man of few words. Perhaps he was not so fluent in English. He was not given to expressing his finer emotions in English particularly, unlike Shalini. At times she switched to Malayalam. In whatever manner she spoke, he listened to her with rapt attention. The feel he had was indescribable, as his paragon of perfection sat beside him, leaning on his broad shoulders. He wished for this journey to never see its end.

As their vehicle sped towards its destination, Shalini enjoyed the sights of the outskirts of Delhi. They alighted to visit some famous tombs early on the tour. Why, Shalini wondered, did the early Mughal rulers give so much importance to these memorials for their dead? Even the Taj was a great tomb, built in memory of Mumtaz Mahal. They believed that memories outlived the dead. These tombs were the everlasting symbols of the fond memories of their dear departed, they believed. Shalini had a disturbing thought. What if they were destroyed by a natural calamity, like an earthquake? The whole edifice would be in shambles. What should happen to the 'everlasting symbol' of love then? It was a depressing thought. She realised that Love can exist only in spirit, and not in its physical form for very long. The Taj had enshrined the love shared by two individuals in their spirit. Long after they were dead and gone, people looked upon the Taj as proof of the deathless love that they had had for each other, epitomised by this inspiring building. All such feelings crowded her mind as they sped towards their destination.

Would her feelings for Chandran grow into something similar? Shalini felt that she was perhaps romanticizing the Taj a bit too much. She took a peek at Chandran seated next to her. He did not seem to be troubled by any such imaginings, except that he was gazing at her in rapt admiration. Shalini was more excited and thrilled by the very thought that she was going out on such an interesting trip for the first time with a young man whom she liked so much.

They alighted near the sprawling gardens and lawns around the Taj just before sunset. They had some coffee and snacks at a nearby stall before entering the gardens. The weather had been warm and comfortable so far, but as dusk approached, it started to get cooler. It promised to be a starry and moonlit night ahead. On enquiry, Chandran understood that the last bus back to Delhi was at nine and they decided not to miss it, though she secretly wished that they would stay overnight at some place near the Taj Mahal. She did not, however, insist on it. She had decided to take their affair, which she believed it was, one step at a time. She knew Chandran was a morally cautious sort of a person. It would not have been a good idea for her to push him into committing himself. Slowly, along with the other tourists who had come to watch the Taj by moonlight, they moved towards the historic building. Just as she had overheard, the effect was magical. The pure white and picturesque building was bathed in the soft glow of the moon that had now risen above. The strange play of shadows over the reflecting surfaces, along with the silent river flowing past the marble monument, created an uncanny effect for the viewers. They went around the building once with the other viewers. By the next round, they found themselves alone, apart from the rest of the crowd.

They found themselves standing in a corner, in the shadow of one of the minarets, looking down upon the waters of the river flowing past. Shalini snuggled closer to Chandran as the atmosphere had turned quite cool. Suddenly, without a warning, Chandran swept her into his arms, kissing her deeply and with great urgency. She responded quite naturally, a deep and satisfying kiss for both of them having been starved of a physical contact with each other. She had eagerly been waiting for some such gesture from him. The moonlight played havoc with their passions. For him, it came with great intensity, as his eager lips planted his seal of desire on her warm and responding face. It was such a release for all his pent-up feelings towards her that he had kept under tight control over all these years. For her, it was the fruition of the great yearning she felt for him whenever he came close to her. Perhaps, this stamp of their silent union was witnessed by the spirits of Shah Jahan and Mumtaz, who would definitely have blessed them. A few moments later, they surfaced from their passionate embrace and kiss. Chandran looked deep into her eyes and spoke breathlessly, "Darling, my dear little Shalu, forgive me. I could not control myself. All these days, I have been longing to do just this. I love you so much! But I couldn't find the courage to express myself. I wondered whether you would take it amiss."

"Shh…don't you apologise, Chandru. Do not break this magic. This was the best gift you could give me at the Taj. Why this delay? I must have loved you from the first moment I set eyes on you, many years ago. The feeling was confirmed when I met you again in Delhi. I have been longing for some intimate moments with you since then. I am so happy we came here."

He did not allow her to continue. She was once more overpowered in a tight embrace and an even more intimate kiss. His hands groped her figure, as she moulded herself into his willing hands. As they stood savouring this first heady experience, they suddenly became conscious of their surroundings. Silently thanking the Taj for a long-desired release of their bottled up feelings towards each other, they moved away from the deep shadows and joined the other tourists in their journey back. After a hurried dinner at a nearby restaurant, they caught the last bus back to Delhi. This trip to the Taj had now become unforgettable for Shalu. It must have been so for Chandru also, judging by the amusingly bewildered expression on his face. She caught him gazing at her with tenderness and love from time to time. As for her, words could not express the feeling of deep sensuous satisfaction she felt, when he thus reciprocated her love and longing for him.

When the bus dropped them off at a stop near her university campus, he had his car ready nearby. He dropped her off near her hostel inside the campus and gave her a goodnight kiss with a simple peck on her cheeks. Promising to meet in one or two days, he drove back to his place.

Chapter 5
Future Plans

Back at her hostel, Shalu realised that sleep was hard at arriving. Her romantic fancies took wing. Was Chandru aware of the significance of this trip for both of them? As for her, she felt quite clear that she loved this quiet, intense man with all her heart. She sensed that it was a love that knew no barriers of caste, community or religion. It was an ancient passionate longing for her chosen soul-mate that ignored the past and present obstacles; one that swept over time and their own helpless selves consumed with passion, in its hurtling tides. Just being with him had become a yearning need. He was her timeless lover, her Krishna, her hero Arjuna, her Nala, and a host of all other characters he enacted. He was her physical, emotional and spiritual essence and anchor. She loved his body and soul, his handsome physique, as well as his mind and spirit. In her wildest imaginations, his real self took on the contours of all the mythical figures he represented on stage, raising him to an elevated level, giving him a divine allure. Was her imagination running wild? In this moment, she believed that he would never let her down, that she deserved him for her steadfast devotion to him. She did not realize when her tired eyes folded in to a deep slumber.

As for Chandran, he was overcome with a deep sense of fulfilment. He could not believe that his secret love had been rewarded after all these years in the most unexpected manner.

To meet her, his dream girl, after so many years, to be able to be intimate with her, take her on a trip to the Taj, and to find fruition for his deep sense of longing for her at the historic place – these were matters he could never have imagined before. He was humbled by the thought that such a high born and desirable lady could find something so precious in him to love and cherish. He decided to do his utmost to earn and be worthy of this love. Their next meeting was scheduled for two days later. Both of them wanted to meet more frequently now. The yearning to be close to each other despite all obstacles was unmistakable.

At their next meeting two days later, they relived their past again which brought back all their hidden feelings for each other. They had not admitted the presence of such emotions even to themselves, till that very moment. The fear of public censure had overcome everything else in their minds. Now, however, the glorious freedom to choose and indulge in their sensuous love for each other overwhelmed them. They did not lose even a minute opportunity in avowing the attraction and intense passion that they had for each other. It was painful when they had to part even for a few days for matters concerning their respective studies. She, in her research for her PhD, and he, in his job that often took him to various parts of India, as well as abroad. She decided to speed up her PhD work, concentrating on assembling the material that she had collected. She wanted to complete it within a year. She even hoped to land a job at a local college after the completion of her PhD, which was one of the required and most important qualifications for the job.

Chandran, meanwhile, was taken up with the organising of the annual Kathakali 'Mela' which was to be put up in different parts of India, as also at important cultural centres within the capital. At some centres, competitions were announced between the various groups of major Kathakali actors. It was Chandran's wish to excel along with his friends and co-workers when competing against the other performers, to bring credit to his Institute. Shalini was lucky to be able to attend the first performance at a nearby centre. She had been busy for a while with the final work of submitting her thesis. They had not met for a couple of months. Since Chandran had sent her a free pass, she was able to sit in the front row along with the V.I.Ps and foreign dignitaries who had come specially on invitation. She eagerly awaited his performance.

The first mythical story enacted was that of Nala and Damayanti, the scene where Damayanti is separated from Nala in the forest. The soulful rendering of the songs and Chandran's '*abhinaya*' as Nala brought tears to her eyes. She observed that a few discerning among the audience were also emotionally caught up thus. She wished with all her heart to never have to part with Chandran once they got married, unlike the hapless Damayanthi in that scene. The next act to be depicted on stage was the scene of '*Doothu*' from the Mahabharata. Chandran excelled on stage as Sri Krishna, bargaining with the Kauravas for a meagre piece of land for his cousins, the Pandavas. After the show, she dropped in on him at the greenroom. In all the majesty of the Kathakali '*vesham*' of Sri Krishna, the sight of him overwhelmed her. He, however, seemed to be in a totally different world, barely acknowledging her presence. People had crowded around him, congratulating him one after the other. Shalu quickly slipped past him and returned to her hostel.

Lying back in her bed, with sleep refusing to descend, Shalini was reminded of another time, another stage, where a similar thing had happened. She had gone backstage to meet Chandran, before he took down his dress and makeup. She had the shock of her life when she observed the figure of Chandran as Sri Krishna, standing in a corner and casually smoking a cigarette! When Chandran noticed her approaching, he had hurriedly thrown away his cigarette before turning to her and saying, "Shalu, what are you doing here? I told you not to meet me when I am in my Kathakali outfit here in the greenroom. Why couldn't you wait outside for me?"

He was always opposed to revealing his feelings for her in public. Shalini knew this. There was an innate shyness in him that made it almost impossible for him to reveal his deeper feelings to her. She was the exact opposite, however. She never tired of showing her affection and appreciation for him whenever it caught her fancy. It was a spontaneous reaction for her. She did not bother about the people around her or his embarrassment with being in full view of the public. As she went closer to him, he backed off.

"Hey! What do you want? Don't come any nearer. Do not touch me, my make-up will spread and become unsightly. I'll take it off and come to you in a minute."

Shalini had wanted to get close to him, and maybe even touch him in his made-up form. She whispered hoarsely, "But I want to be near you, Chandru, to feel you, to know that you are a real person, to know that you are mine, the man behind the mask. I feel so proud of you whenever I witness such a wonderful applause for you. Please tell me that you acknowledge my feelings."

"Oh! dear, is this the time and place for all this? Keep your distance, please," he whispered back.

He then surprised her when he said in a serious tone, "As an actor, a performer, I belong to no one. I become one with the character. The outside world no longer exists for me. I become Nala, I am Sri Krishna, or whoever the character is in the story enacted. I take this attitude on to give the best to my role. At that moment, you become just one among my various admirers, perhaps the favourite one."

Shalini reacted with shock at this unexpected disclosure. She could not understand this objective distancing of Chandran from everything and everybody in the outside world during his time on stage. It was quite disturbing for her, a creature of spontaneous outbursts. So, he forgot all about their intimate moments when he donned his make-up. This quality might have made him a great performer, but in her eyes, a little less of a lover. She had vainly tried to read the emotion in his frighteningly intense eyes at that moment, but the depth of his expression evaded her. This episode had repeated itself yet again this day. She had had enough of Kathakali for the moment, she thought as she cried herself to sleep. She had decided to ignore him for the next few days. Didn't she have some self-respect too?

A few days later, Chandran came knocking at her door. He seemed to have forgotten his behaviour towards her the last time they had met. His busy schedule was over for now. He wanted her to go out with him. He pleaded with her, but she was not one to forget the slight that easily. It finally dawned on him that she had taken offence at his attitude from before. He literally begged her to excuse him for his selfish behaviour, as she had described it. He had reverted to his former charming and winning self.

"My dear Shalu, how could you have misunderstood my words? You saw how I was hailed as the most successful Kathakali artist? That's only because I am totally committed to the work at hand. I am so involved in the character and the situations I am enacting, that anything outside of it seems as an obstacle in my successful portrayal of the character. So please, forgive me. I had felt a little taken aback by your demands that day, I was not prepared for your overture, but I was far from rejecting you." He looked sheepish and awkward. "The public display of your admiration put me off. Don't you see? I do not want people to talk behind our backs and create a sleazy scandal," he continued in a beseeching tone.

Shalini could not give up her stand all at once, and said, "How could you have rejected my presence? I just wanted a mere contact, an assurance that you did consider me above everybody else. But you chose to ignore me and hurt me with your speech." She paused. "There is a time and place for all this, isn't it?" she mimicked his words. "So, now the time has come?"

The sarcasm was not lost on him. He was at his persuasive best. "Look here, Shalu. I told you, I am not happy with what occurred. How can I possibly make up for it?" With an impish expression, he continued, "Do you want me to come in a 'total Kathakali' attire to arouse you? But that will take time, won't it? And it would be really messy – first the facial mask will come off, then the crown, and then the starched dress. It would be an incongruous sight."

She laughed out loud as she imagined the spectacle. The humour of the situation had managed to strike her, lightening the moment immediately. Chandran heaved a sigh of relief. He also had the grace to look ashamed and laugh away the mental image he had created of himself to win his argument.

"I do not mean it to be a meaningless demonstration. I just wanted to feel the magic of your performance, I longed for a reciprocating gesture from you when I wanted to touch you backstage; some small gesture to show me that you understood my empathy and admiration for the character you played. It would have allowed me to at least be a part of your performance mentally."

Chandran's voice beamed with affection as he began, "I know, dear. When you dashed backstage that day, it was a bit unexpected and overwhelming for me. Anyway, here I am now – I am putty in your hands, but only in the privacy of our homes. You can express your admiration for me in whatever way you deem fit." He said it with a twinkle in his eyes, which made her blush. He gathered her into his arms, and the rest was sheer bliss for Shalu. Despite her desires to the contrary, Chandru, being naturally cautious and traditional, never went all the way. He believed that they should 'give their all to each other' only after marriage. Though Shalu was not averse to a bit of experimentation in love, she gave in to his persuasion and had to comfort herself with the titbits he doled out to her in his outbursts of passion.

They decided to celebrate by going to their favourite South Indian restaurant, where they had 'masala dosa' and fruit juice. When Chandran dropped her off at her hostel later, she felt truly exhausted. She was soon going to submit her thesis and knew that she would not be able to continue at the hostel indefinitely after that. She decided to rent a small flat at a place which was more economical. This meant moving away from Chandran's place. Though disappointed at first, Chandran reassured her that once his immediate commitments were over, they would seriously think about tying the knot. Meanwhile, she could take up a one-year certificate course in teaching, which would benefit her later when she would apply for a lecturer's post too. She could land a job only after being awarded her PhD though. She immediately accepted this suggestion, as she was ready to do anything to be near Chandran. There was more than a month for the course to start, so she decided to take a well-earned vacation for herself. She decided to go back to her parents, and if possible, to her native place too, of which she had so many treasured memories.

When informed of her plans, Chandran also became enthusiastic for her sake. He told her that in a few days, he would be due for his vacation too. He would go back to his native place in Malabar, and asked Shalini whether she could make it there as well. She promised him to think about it. On this note, they agreed to separate for the present.

Chapter 6

Catching Up

Shalu reached her parents' home in three days by train. She had about four weeks before joining the teaching and computer course she had applied for, which was to keep her occupied till she was awarded her PhD. Her home was in the capital city. Her brother had come to pick her up from the station. The very next day at home, she woke up late. She loved lingering lazily in bed, well past her usual wake up time. Finally, she got up as she heard her mother calling out stringently, "Shalini, do get up! It is after ten in the morning!"

She tried to get up, but curled up once more into her bed spread, till she was awakened by her mother's continuous calls and dire musings. "Oh God, how will she manage on her own after marriage! If she gets up only by ten o'clock, how will she adjust to the needs of her new home, husband and kids? I wonder what they'll get for breakfast. They will have to go hungry most days, if she decides to sleep thus!"

As she got up, she shot back with a fitting reply, "Don't worry, mom. We'll then have a continental breakfast." Smiling at her mother's bewildered expression, she added, "Oh, we'll survive."

"Continental breakfast, my foot! That is only an excuse for your laziness over making traditional South Indian items like idly and dosa for breakfast. What if you end up getting married to a conservative Kerala Brahmin who cannot miss his 'desi' breakfast?"

"Well, I shall wean him away from his traditional preferences and bring him around to like cornflakes, bread, fruit and milk."

"High hopes you have of transforming an average Malayali into such a person of your imagination! I wonder how a person can survive on cornflakes daily! It tastes just like '*thavidu*' (husk)! How do millions look forward to those dry tasteless baked maida bricks!" Her mother's distaste for cornflakes and bread was quite evident.

"You just have to get used to them," Shalini gently teased her mother for her lack of knowledge of the world outside, her preference for traditional food and vegetarian fare, and her reluctance to modernize her taste buds by trying out the 'modern dishes' as she called them with derision.

"At this rate, how will you ever come and stay with me if I decide to settle in Delhi? You'll have to get used to a minimum of South Indian vegetables and rice. I prefer those 'modern new-fangled dishes', mom."

Her mother gave her a meaningful glare, perhaps hinting that she would deal with the matter when she actually came to face it in future. Shalini chose to drop the topic then, but her list of complaints was far from over.

"It is your Delhi stay that has made you so ultramodern. I wish you had stayed back here to study. Is the change in your dressing and food habits all there is for you to reveal to us? Or do you have other dark secrets too?" Her mother looked at her suspiciously.

How close she was to the truth, thought Shalini.

She hastened to add, "Dear mom, beneath all this alleged modernity, I am still the same old Shalini, do not fear. I am still a vegetarian. I just gave up the sari and other South Indian dresses for churidars, jeans, leggings and tops, as they are more convenient to wear there."

Her affair with Chandran would still have to remain an 'undercover operation'. She knew that her tradition-bound parents would never accept her relationship at that point in time. It would take time to make them understand that their daughter's happiness depended on a man whom they would hesitate to associate with, given the conventional attitude of their community, despite all the education and social progress.

Shalini became more discreet and devious in her plans of joining Chandran at her native place in Malabar. The less her parents had any inkling of her activities, the better it was for her. Only an unexpected and shocking action on her part later might force them to give in to her wishes, she thought, and make them give their blessings for her life with her precious Chandran. But again, that was something she would have to worry about in future.

Shalini reflected on her immediate background, especially that of her parents. Her mother was a simple, plump, fair, middle aged woman, indulgent towards her children as long as they did not cross her path. She had a soft corner for her son like any average Indian mother, also because he was the youngest. This had led to occasional outbursts and fights against her younger brother when Shalini had been quite young herself. She often complained of her mother's 'partiality' towards her brother. Now that she had become older and more mature, the sibling rivalry had died down. She now affectionately indulged and entertained him. Perhaps since she had someone more important to focus on now, she felt quite tolerant of her younger brother Ravi and his antics. Earlier she considered Ravi no more than a mischievous brat. Now, he seemed to be a little less irritating to her.

Shalini had brought him a gift of some of his favourite sports gear. He used to play some occasional shuttle, badminton and cricket with his friends. He was glad when she presented him with the sports items. He was tall for his age, well-built and bubbling with vitality. He had many friends, unlike Shalini. He had begun to sprout a moustache too, she observed.

"Look at the junior man in the house!" she couldn't help commenting. "Don't you have many admirers, including girls, Ravi? I bet you string them along."

"No, sis." He looked embarrassed. "Perhaps a few good friends only."

"You see, since ours is a professional college, there aren't many pretty faces there. But there's an Arts College for women nearby. There we spot a few better looking ones. I get my share of adulation from some beauties there." He was preening himself, making himself a hero of an imagined situation.

"Be careful, don't fall for an immature idiot. Don't you want a sensible woman in your life, Ravi?"

"Who wants sense in a beautiful girl?" Ravi echoed the typical sentiments of a chauvinistic twenty-year old male of their community. As he was fond of music and dance, he wanted the girl of his choice to have good taste in music and other performing arts. He loved to dance to the beats of western music.

"Don't expect to come across a girl well versed in western numbers, Ravi. Here, of all the places too. You might have a chance in Delhi or Bombay, perhaps."

"Enough with your praise of Delhi! Mind you, once I complete my studies, I shall definitely try for a job in Delhi or Bombay. Or, perhaps even go to a foreign country. So don't brag about Delhi too much." His obvious envy regarding her 'privileged' stay in the capital city was quite evident to her.

"And you'd end up marrying a 'phoren' girl, I bet," she teased him.

"Never! Running around with such girls is fun. But when I settle down, I'll definitely marry and settle down with a quiet, shy, homely girl chosen by our parents."

Well, thought Shalini, her brother was a typical Momma and Papa's darling, obedient and sensitive to the demands and expectations of their parents.

"How about you, sis? Whom do you want to be your life–partner?"

"Well, I only know that I want to marry a clean–shaven, good man."

"Clean shaven? In the south, men with moustaches are considered to be macho. Don't you know, sis? It must be the influence of Delhi on you, I bet. In these parts of Kerala, you will have to get hooked with some Kathakali or Bharatanatyam performer to get a clean-shaven man as a husband."

Shalini was taken aback at this comment. If only he knew how close to the truth he was. She resolved to keep her real choice totally hidden till she could make them accept the inevitable. She knew it would come as a shock to them, and decided to wait till the initial crisis of their marriage, which would be an unacceptable one to her parents, was blown over, before she announced their relationship to them and to the rest of the world. She recognised the rebel in herself, who refused to bow down to the conventions dictated by her community and society in general. She decided to be all the more discreet in all her future actions.

Her father wanted to know how she had fared in her PhD interview – it was an open defence – and was glad to find out that she had done well.

"Why don't you apply to some local colleges here after you are awarded with the PhD degree? If you're interested, you can apply at government colleges as well, though you might get a transfer to some far of place initially."

When Shalini did not reply, he understood that she was not too keen at the idea.

"You are so taken up with Delhi that you want to pursue a job there, isn't it?"

She nodded in assent. She did not want to appear too eager. "Perhaps a little later. It is like this, father. There, I find myself in the midst of an International community with more exposure. The campus itself was such an eye opener. If I am offered a really challenging job in Delhi, I may decide to settle there. I might put in an application for a job here in time too."

She did not want them to get suspicious. She was only trying to prepare them in case she settled down in Delhi. Her father looked at her quizzically and said, "If you so prefer Delhi for a career, I have no objection to it, dear. It is only your mother who has a difference of opinion about this. Naturally, she wants you working closer to our place here."

Her father realised that Shalini had grown more confidant, smart and knowledgeable after having gone to Delhi for her higher studies. She would never have been so fearless to walk the streets, even in the dark, had she been staying here. She had also learned to handle the car with absolute ease. He was proud of her daughter and her achievements, but he dared not voice these feelings in front of his wife.

"Why can't she marry and settle down here, now that her studies are over?" her mother kept repeating. "It will be easier to search for a suitable boy in our own community, if she comes back here."

"There's no dearth of educated boys from our community back in Delhi either. I'll just have to contact some of my friends there once we start searching. But first, let her give us her consent over it, so that we may actually start looking for a good boy," Shalini's father assured her mother.

"I don't want to hear such excuses. Let us take her birth chart to some reputed astrologer and get it tallied with that of some local boy of our preference. I wish to see her married off without much delay. She's not growing any younger, you know."

Her father did not respond to these concerns of her mother immediately. Shalini overheard her mother's tirade with trepidation. She had to intervene before they became any more serious about this matter.

"Mother, I do not want to get married before I land a job, either here or at Delhi. That's definite. So please postpone your match making plans, Mom."

Her mother stared at her in reluctant wonder.

"Well, well! See how our daughter takes her own decisions! In my younger days, it was a matter of honour to get married by eighteen, and daughters never went against the words of their parents. There was no question of any more studies after that either."

"These are not your times, Devi. Our daughter is a highly qualified lady now. It would be a pity if she did not hold a good job in keeping with her achievements. After she gets a job, I'll have to be careful in selecting a boy to her liking. It'll have to be a boy who does not object to her being so educated and gainfully employed."

Shalini heaved a sigh of relief. At least her father understood her and supported her in her decision of having a job. He did not want to marry her off in a hurry.

"That's what I meant, father. If you had wanted me to settle down when I was eighteen or nineteen, then why did you take the trouble of educating me so much at all? You could have 'married me off at eighteen' and be done with it." She mimicked her mother's tone.

Her father laughed out loud.

"That settles it, Devi. There's no need to rush things. Let her, if she so wishes, go back and try getting a job in Delhi first.

We'll think about a suitable alliance for her when she is ready to marry." His tone rang with a finality which brooked no arguments from her mother's side. Her mother knew a lost case when she saw one. Shalini thanked her stars that this critical moment was past.

She knew that her mother was not too pleased, and did not pursue the topic any further. However, Shalini sensed that her mother would certainly take up the subject again some time in future. She was just biding her time.

It was always her father who supported her in taking these bold decisions. Would his reaction be the same if he came to know the real reason behind her decision, she wondered. She did not want to dwell on any unpleasant consequences at present. She whiled away her time there visiting her old haunts in and around the city. She dropped in at the school she had studied, met some of her old teachers who were delighted to see her, went on to visit the college where she had graduated from and even met a few of her friends who stayed near her college. Most of them had gotten married and settled down in life. They made fun of her for delaying her marriage. If only they knew! She dared not open up to them for fear that her parents might somehow come to know of her affair with Chandran.

She wandered once more through the huge public library that had helped her get through her PG with flying colours. City life was not conducive to long friendships, mused Shalini. Social life for her parents, in a broad sense, was almost zero. They belonged to the so called 'higher caste and class' which refused to mingle with the other sections of the society. They lived in an ivory tower. This clannish and snobbish nature of their behaviour was displayed best at social functions and public events. Shalini had developed a hatred for such social gatherings, like weddings, where people of her community showed such discrimination towards other people belonging to lower castes and classes. All hell would have broken loose if her affair with Chandran had come to public notice at that point in time. Her liking and attraction towards Chandran might be an unconscious rebellion against her narrow minded community members, Shalini felt.

Once she grew up and became more educated and aware of the undercurrents in such relationships, Shalini gave up attending the social functions, such as marriages, along with her parents within her community. She believed that people benefitted from such social interactions only if they were followed up by generous actions of unbiased give and take. They should keep warm contacts and help each other and the society in general, unlike the self-centred hypocrites she met during these societal gatherings. Her family still kept up appearances, though her father did not enjoy such things. Shalini knew that if she was forced to blend in, she might. For the time being, however, she enjoyed being independent in her attitude and views, including her relationship with Chandran, which she was not ready to expose yet.

Soon after, Chandran phoned her up late one night, as she had given him her parents' landline number, when her parents had luckily gone out with her brother for a late-night movie show. He informed her that he would come down to Kerala in a week, specifying a date for the next week. He assured her that he would try and contact her when he arrived. He would be at his home in Malabar at that time and would form further plans when they met.

"Longing to see you, dear. I miss you so much." There was a certain intensity in his voice that Shalini loved.

"I am also anxious to be near you, dear," she reciprocated with equal passion. "I'll try and make it to the *tharavad* from my parents' home at the earliest."

The next day during breakfast, she introduced the topic ambiguously.

"Father, I wish I could see my grandfather's house, our *tharavad,* once again. Who stays there now? I had some jolly good times in that big house when I was a little girl."

Though her father seemed taken aback at this sudden wish from his grown daughter, he seemed pleased. "Well, the *tharavad* was inherited by my elder brother, your *Valiyachan*. He lives there with his family. Since the death of your grandparents, we have never visited him there. Of course, we keep contact when we meet at social functions."

"I have fond memories of the place from our vacations there when I was younger. Those happy innocent games I used to play with so many of my cousins, roaming about in the mangroves, and plucking and devouring raw mangoes, I remember it all. I can never forget the experience of watching the '*Malayarattu*' in awe, and the memorable all-night Kathakali performances."

Her father looked at her in growing wonder and a wee bit of pride. He tried hard to conceal it from his wife, as she did not have much respect for her in-laws who lived there.

"You still remember those times, dear? Well, there hasn't been a Kathakali or *theyyam* performance there for years, but those woods and the mangroves and the distant river are still there. I was under the impression that you and your brother would never relish going to the rustic countryside again. That is why we never insisted that you accompany us even when we went there during the death rites of your grandparents. Of course, you had exams then and could not afford to miss classes too. And then, it is such a long way off as well."

"But I long to see the place one more time, father, for a few days at least, before the pristine beauty of the place is destroyed by modernisation."

"Well, if you really want to go visit, I can arrange for it. I'll contact *Ettan* (brother) and inform him. Either he or one of his children, you know he has two boys, will definitely come to pick you up at the station. I do not have any leave to spare, otherwise I would have accompanied you there myself."

Overriding any objections that her mother could have put across, her father was determined to let her visit his homeland and the *tharavad*.

"You have come here after so long, and you want to spend more time with your uncle and aunt than with us?" Her mother did not fail to voice her complaint.

"Do let me go, mother. I long for a respite from the hustle-bustle of cities. What better place could there be for me to visit, than the remote countryside that father lived in? At least, it won't be a strange new place for me. I have relatives there who will take care of all my needs."

"How can you go to such a place alone? Let your brother accompany you and drop you there, at least."

"Oh no, mother. I can go by myself. I shall be fine, as long as father can arrange for someone to come pick me up at the railway station."

Her mother reluctantly agreed. Her father wanted her to have one more vacation of her choice to his own native place. He had confidence in her capacity to travel alone and take care of herself. He informed his brother's family about her trip and booked a ticket for her in the first class compartment of a train bound for the northern destination.

Chapter 7

Countryside Pleasures

Shalini was soon off on her journey to the north of Kerala. She felt bad about not confiding in them the truth of her rendezvous with Chandran. All in good time, she reflected. This daytime train journey, from the southern end of Kerala to the northern end, was something she dearly cherished. She was lucky to have got a window seat. The view from the window, the glorious verdant greenery, typical of the Kerala landscape, rolled out its silky green carpet of fields on either side of the railroad. It was broken at places by stretches of jagged hills, or the beautiful backwaters that appeared whenever they passed over a bridge. At times, they passed over a river flowing passively along, while at other times, she could see an overflowing river with its onrush of perilous waters. There were mountain ranges in a distance. She could see the spirals or *gopurams* of temples from afar, as the train sped past them. Occasionally, she spotted cattle feeding on green pastures, or devotees taking a dip in the rivers, or the tanks or ponds of nearby temples. She felt herself rising in spirit towards the swaying fronds of coconut palms that soothe the eyes of any Keralite travelling through any part of the world. Quite a contrast it was to the arid and scorching plains that greeted her when she was bound to the northern parts of the country, especially Delhi.

The sheer breath-taking beauty of the landscape never failed to raise a fierce sense of pride in her. For a moment, she regretted having to leave her native homeland to settle in Delhi. She was content to let her eyes wander over the sights of the wild, untamed countryside. She never tired of watching the familiar sight of labourers in the paddy fields, bending down knee deep in water, engaged in planting the seeds during the sowing season. The sight of their healthy children, with dark but glowing skin which gleamed in the sunlight, playing in the grounds nearby, pleased her. When the train passed through the local towns, it bustled with the sound of new people. She began observing the varied crowds from other parts of the state with interest. She became aware of the different locales by listening closely to their language, which differed in the use of the local slang. Having had her lunch, which her mother had judiciously packed for her, she dozed off a little. By the time she woke up, it was almost evening and she had come very close to her destination.

This train journey made Shalini wonder about the many contradictions of her life. Here she was, an upper middle-class woman, born and brought up in a conservative and aristocratic background in Kerala, exposed to the cream of the academic society in Delhi, containing the confluence of varied cultures, now journeying back to her roots - back to the countryside, shedding all the earlier prejudices of her community and society. This was a new Shalini, full of expectations and hope for a better future for both Chandran and herself, where she could rise above the limitations set by the conservative attitude of the people there. She was pleased with herself for being able to see a former dependent as an equal, to be able to understand him, to love him and to long for his presence. Despite the rejection and shock that she would surely face from her parents at this bold choice, she had not one moment of regret with regard to Chandran. He was a gentleman. He could sense her slightest wish and tried to get it done, as long as it was within his means.

As she sat observing the sights and sounds from the speeding train, lines from one of her favourite Hindi movies from the seventies rose in her mind – she loved humming tunes in a moving train – and unconsciously escaped her lips,

"Jo tumko ho pasand,
Wohi baat kahenge,
Tum dinko agar raat
Kaho, raat kahenge."

The sound of her humming got lost in the sounds of the rattling train. The lover in the movie assures the heroine with this song that whatever she wanted, he would surely follow suit. What a great lover he was! She wanted Chandran to be such an ideal lover, as she was sure he would turn out to be.

She suddenly noticed some commotion going on inside the compartment which sounded like an argument over a seat. The concerned people were talking on top of their voices. As Shalini could not follow the issue precisely, she riveted her gaze back to the scenes out of her window and took another sip of the coffee she had just purchased. She definitely did prefer watching the trees and tall buildings at a distance, silhouetted against the setting sun. The journey was coming to a close for her.

Her uncle had been waiting for her at the station. He was overjoyed upon meeting her. It had been a long time since he saw her last. She was glad to see him after such a gap too. He took her back in his car to the place where he lived with his family. It was a forty five minutes' drive back to the old *tharavad*.

"How was the journey, *molutty*?" That was how her uncle always addressed her affectionately.

"It was okay. Are my cousins home right now? I see this place hasn't changed much over the years," she observed from the car window.

"That is so, but I have made some changes in the interior of the big house. I have made it smaller and more liveable for us. I am surprised that you chose to spend some time here, Shalini."

"I just wanted to get the feel of my favourite places here once more, *Valyacha*. I get nostalgic thinking about the good times I have had here as a young girl."

"Good that you came here at this time. There is a local temple festival going on at the Krishna temple nearby. I shall take you to watch the famous '*Thidambu Nritham*' connected with the temple ceremonies."

"Oh, I shall find my way around." She realized that they were nearing the ancient homestead when the lights of the township got left behind. She could not observe the scenery around anymore, as it had gotten dark. Both her uncle's children, the boys, were studying in distant places and were staying at their college hostels. Thus, her uncle and aunt were staying alone at the big house at that moment, with one or two servants to help them out. They soon entered a brightly lit portico. She saw her aunt emerging from the entrance with a welcoming smile on her face. She was a matronly lady, unlike her tall and lean uncle.

"Did you have a good journey? Come on, have a cup of coffee and snacks with us. Dinner will be ready in an hour or two. Make yourself comfortable."

Her aunt presented a picture of efficiency as she bustled about the house. After unpacking and having her coffee, Shalini looked around to see what changes her uncle had brought about in the old building. The huge three storey'd building, with its long veranda, or '*nadapura*' as it was called, with the open courtyard, or '*naalukettu*' - a space surrounded by four pillars, beyond the entrance, still seemed intact. The huge decorative pillars that supported the roof of the entrance and portico still held up the building in all its fading glory. These parts were just as she remembered them to have been. The entrance passage led to a small living area, beyond which was situated the courtyard and other rooms. In the renovation work done by her uncle, she saw that he had shortened the extensive corridor within. Some of the extra rooms had been demolished, and the rest were made more compact and liveable. The addition of neat, modern tiled bathrooms attached to the existing bedrooms was a great relief. The flooring was also redone in beautiful marble tiles. On the whole, it looked very impressive. She voiced her appreciation to her uncle for his effort to modernise the place.

"Do you still have the big pond, *Valyacha*(uncle)? I used to love swimming in it."

"Oh yes, dear. We could not destroy it as we still use it for religious functions, when conducting *shraddha,* etc."

Shalini looked forward to bathing in the waters of her favourite pond once again.

"But you should avoid using it after it gets dark. You can never be too sure of the slimy creatures within that proliferate in the shadow of darkness."

She nodded in agreement to the timely warning by her uncle.

"I will show you your room. Why don't you freshen up a bit? I shall serve the dinner soon."

After cleaning up, she returned to the part which served as a dining room, an extension of the living room. There was a big TV with cable connection there. Her uncle was listening to the evening news. So, she thought, she need not miss some of her favourite programmes if they were aired in this part of the state. She sat down on one of the chairs of the settee provided in front of the TV and relaxed.

An hour later, they sat down to dinner. Shalini relished the homely meals served by her aunt. The boiled rice with dal curry - a concoction of dal, pepper and seasonal vegetables typical to that area - tasted absolutely delicious. It was rounded off with some fresh curd, crunchy *'pappadam'* (a crispy treat, a speciality), and banana chips. It had been so long since Shalini had had the chance to taste all of it.

"Mm…these taste divine, aunty. It has been so long since I've had such a *'naadan'*(countryside special) curry."

'How are your studies getting along? We heard you were doing your PhD?" The query was from her academically oriented Uncle.

"Oh, it is over now, *Valyacha*. I have submitted my thesis. I need to appear for my viva later. Right now, I am just concentrating on enjoying a longed-for holiday."

"What about getting married, Shalu? Should all of us be on the look-out for a suitable boy?"

"All in good time, aunty. I'd like to get a job first and work independently for some time. Only then will I think of settling down."

The expression on the face of her aunt, a country-bred woman, was one of disbelief and bewilderment.

"All these modern ideas! At your age, I had already given birth to my son."

"Well, times have changed, dear. Let her have her wish." Her uncle was better at accepting her views. Her father had taken a lot after this quiet, dignified man, felt Shalini.

"What about my cousins? Do they come down during Onam? Do they have holidays?"

"The elder one, Bhasker, comes down during the *pooja* holidays. He is pursuing his higher studies at Bangalore. The younger one, Shanker, studies at an institution in Coimbatore. He comes here during Diwali."

"It's been ages since I saw them last. Do you have any recent snaps of the two?" Shalini noticed some recent photographs of the children and the parents on a shelf nearby. A snap of the two kids; one, a year or two younger to Shalini, and the other, just a little younger to her own brother.

The whole place was furnished plainly, apart from the modern additions of a dining table, chairs and a side table beside the settee. Shalini could not see any fancy articles on display, unlike at her own house. Her mother, influenced by her artistic father, had decked up their house with rare antiques, a beautiful carpet and a chandelier in the living room. Her aunt was a forthright and plain rustic woman. The atmosphere was likewise plain and practical there.

"Why don't you turn in? You must be tired after the long journey. You can take the room I showed you earlier on the northern side," said her aunt, with a hint of concern in her voice.

The room allotted to her was a comfortably large room, which had, besides the double bed and small side tables, a big writing table and a chair. There was a dressing table and a mirror situated in one corner. There was also an attached bathroom. The wall on one side had a built-in shelf. She reflected that the room was either used as a guest bedroom, or it belonged to one of the boys. There was a large window on one wall which opened out to the outside of the house. It was kept locked at that moment, as it was night time. Usually she had trouble falling asleep at a new place, but that day, she slept soundly, perhaps due to the exhaustion from the long journey. Before hitting the bed, she gave a call to Chandran and her parents on their landline and informed them of her safe arrival. To a curious aunt, she explained that she had to phone a concerned friend, giving the number here. He told her that he would get back to her sometime the next day, after he planned out their future meetings.

She woke up at daybreak the next morning and left the house to have a good look around. There was a small garden outside with plants, flowering trees and fruit trees that had grown wild due to minimum care. There were mango and jackfruit trees with their shady branches, flowers plants and trees like the hibiscus, jasmine, bougainvillea and a few others that she did not know the names of. She could not help but compare it with the well-kept garden maintained by her parents back home in the city. Beyond the two acres of land around the main house, all that she could see was untamed woods and hills. Far in the distance, she could see the mountains, ranges of the Western Ghats, which formed a picturesque background. She decided to go exploring up there with Chandran, if it would be convenient for him. She knew that there was a river somewhere down there, near the mountain slopes.

As the first step, she decided to have a bath and a good swim in the big pond near the homestead. Soon after her bath and a refreshing swim in the clear waters, she came back to the house for breakfast. After informing her concerned aunt, she went off on a jaunt in the woods. She visited the family temple there. The temple was surrounded on all sides by woods. It was situated at the foot of a hill covered in mango, coconut, and areca-nut palms trees. These were the very same woods she had frequented with her cousins as a child. It brought back nostalgic memories to her mind.

For instance, this was where her first meeting with Chandran as a fourteen year-old boy had taken place, in the midst of a group of local boys, who, like her cousins and herself, had come to pluck mangoes in the woods. But, since the latter group, including herself, belonged to the aristocratic higher class and caste, they were not allowed to mingle with the other children. Shalini always felt that they could have had such fun together as kids, if it weren't for the caste restrictions. They could only watch the others having fun from a distance.

Drawing herself out of her memories, she devoutly perambulated around the temple three times, and offered a '*vazhipad*' of money to the deity in exchange for a holy dessert of payasam, which she collected from the *poojary*. While returning back from her prayers, she chanced upon a sprawling banyan tree by the side of the temple. When young, it was a habit among her cousins to squat around the '*aalthara*' - the half wall around the banyan tree, and indulge in gossip and other games with each other. She would always become a part of their group whenever she joined them during her vacations. Back in the present, she was tempted to sit on the half wall again and let her mind wander for a bit.

Chapter 8

Pleasure and Passion

When she had informed Chandran of her arrival before starting out from home, she had half expected him to come to the railway station, but she did not meet him there. In hindsight, she realized it was better that he did not turn up there, as her Uncle might have noticed him. Perhaps he would meet her somewhere here, she hoped.

The very next instant, she was surprised and delighted to hear the words, "Shalu, how are you, my dear?" She sprang up from her seat to see Chandran emerge from behind the banyan tree. She was pleasurably surprised to see him so soon.

"Come on, Shalu, let's go someplace more private, where people wouldn't come prying. I know of just such a place in the woods nearby." Chandran urged her to follow him as he led the way onto a woody path.

Shalini quietly followed him. He looked dashing in a lungi and a short sleeved T-shirt, very different from the stiff necked suits she had always seen him in, while in Delhi. He seemed more comfortable here, walking around with a languorous ease. They came to a clearing in the woods, a few metres ahead. On turning right from the main path, they came upon a rocky cave like opening on one side. Chandran led her right into the cave. She was surprised to find that there was space enough inside for two or three people to sit on small and rounded rocky projections. This secluded place was totally hidden from view by the overhanging branches of a huge tree. Shalini wondered why her cousins and she never discovered this cosy secret hiding place during all their wanderings through these woods.

It was the perfect place for their rendezvous. Chandran had already taken his seat on one of the rocks and was dragging her down onto a seat next to his. Chandran held her close. His face lit up with passionate longing.

"Shalu, dear. How I have longed for your presence near me."

He gathered her face close, drawing it towards his own. The next move came as a deep and satisfying kiss. His hands kept probing her, intensifying the passion.

"My dear Shalu, my home is very close this place. One of these days, I shall take you there to meet my mother. Her approval is important for me as far as marriage and settling down is concerned, not that she would have any objection to my wishes."

"But I have only two weeks of vacation left. Remember, I have joined a computer course in Delhi? I'll have to be back before that."

"I know all that. Even a week is enough for me to introduce you to my people and have a memorable vacation with you."

When she looked up at his clean-shaven face, with its row of shining white teeth broadened in an engaging smile, enhanced even more by his intense probing eyes, she felt all the more drawn to him.

"One of these days, perhaps tomorrow, I shall come to your uncle's place pretending to be a friend of yours from Delhi. I shall get his permission to show you around, as I would inform him that I belong to these parts. I shall talk and win him over so well that he will have to agree to let you spend a few hours with me everyday."

She wondered how on earth he was ever going to do that. Her uncle might even agree to it conditionally, but her aunt was far too conservative, oddly curious even about what she considered were Shalini's 'modern ways'. Well, she would see what happened. If not, she would find some other excuse to get outdoors and keep meeting Chandran without arousing their undue suspicions. For the present, she gave herself up to enjoying these precious moments alone with Chandran, and cuddled closer to him.

"You look stunning in the native '*settu mundu*', dear. Much better than when you wear churidars. But of course," he hastened to add, "Whatever you wear for convenience, you look endearing to me nonetheless."

She blushed at the fulsome praise. "You are not far behind either, dear Chandru. You often look ill at ease in your suits and pants in Delhi. This native *mundu*(lungi) with the '*veshti*'(upper cloth) seems much more natural and suitable on you."

Chandran discarded the 'veshti' for better movement, just as she used to give up the shawl of the churidar when in a hurry. Much to Shalini's appreciation, the dark tan on his face took on a deeper hue. This was followed by a deeper and more intense kiss that left Shalini breathless. The pressure of his steely body and muscular arms enfolding her within them, drowned her senses with an expectation for more. But it was Chandran himself who gently disengaged her a few minutes later. The ever practical and self-conscious Chandran kept murmuring to her, "I want you to preserve your best, your sacred virginity, for the night of our wedding day, Shalu, so that the day will be truly memorable."

This, assuming that she was still a virgin, which she was, made Shalini feel that he was quaintly old fashioned. Of course, even she had not had any other male friends till she took up with Chandran. Life at Delhi had not changed his conventional ideas one bit. A few minutes later, having temporarily satiated their yearnings, they took a walk in the woods. As they neared the temple premises, Chandran made away discreetly without a backward glance, just as the priest came into Shalini's view.

"Didn't you leave, madam? I am closing the temple now."

"Oh, I have finished worshipping at the temple. I am just looking around. These places have been familiar to me since my childhood."

He seemed sympathetic towards her. "All these city-bred people, none seem to have a liking for the countryside. You can lead a healthy life if you choose to live here, madam."

"Yes, yes," was all that Shalini could murmur. She pretended to be in haste in order to escape the garrulous old man. She wanted to experience the pleasures of the countryside all by herself, without having to listen to the lectures of a resident. She left the place and took a different path, opposite to the route chosen by Chandran.

She continued her movement through a re-discovery of paths which looked familiar to her. How she wished for Chandran to be with her. By the time she returned to her uncle's house, it was lunch time. After a simple lunch, she retired to her room and curled up with a book on the bed.

True to his word, Chandran came to the *tharavad* that evening. To a curious Uncle, he introduced himself as Shalini's friend from Delhi.

"I belong to these parts, Uncle. When Shalini mentioned about coming here, I decided to look her up. You see, my leave coincided with her vacation. I offered to show her around as a guide. She doesn't remember many of the places here."

Though not fully convinced, despite Chandran mentioning his house name and background, her uncle was relieved that Shalini could now have a male chaperone for her trips.

Otherwise, he did not consider it too safe for a lady to be walking around that place alone.

She heard her uncle calling out to her. "Shalini, do come out. There is somebody who has come to see you."

As she quietly made her way into the outer courtyard, she was pleasantly surprised to see Chandran standing a few feet away, down the steps to the open ground in front of the building. She tried not to look or act too familiar, as did Chandran.

"Here's your friend from Delhi. He is actually a close neighbour of ours here. He belongs to the Nair family living near the temple premises. He belonged to our Kathakali troupe long back. Do you remember his performance as Krishna in the Kathakali dramas we used to conduct here? It was quite famous. Now he says that he is the director of a Kathakali Kendra in Delhi. Quite a rise in life, isn't it?"

"That is where I met him, uncle. Due to my love for Kathakali, I had gone to watch one of the plays staged by his institute. It is near my college hostel premises too. I went backstage to congratulate him. That was when I discovered that he was from around these parts."

"His parents have been our dependents in the past." The arrogance in her uncle's voice was clear to Shalini. She looked apologetically at Chandran, but he did not seem to mind it. He was respectful towards her uncle.

"I am glad that at least this young man has escaped from the situation here and made a name of his own in life," continued her uncle.

Shalini saw her aunt come with a cup of tea for the newcomer. As he stood aside partaking of the tea, her aunt said to him magnanimously, "You can take a seat, Chandran. The old rules from before do not apply now-a-days. Not many show the respect and obeisance that you show to the elderly in these times."

"Old habits die hard, madam. I have been taught right from my childhood to show due respect to the elderly."

He refused to sit in front of them. Shalini sensed that he had turned on the charm for their sake. It was the same concern and unconscious attraction that had made her fall head over heels in love with him, when she had first got acquainted with him in Delhi. Her uncle seemed doubly impressed by his respectful stance.

"How are your folks at home, Chandran? How's your mother coping with her failing health?" her uncle asked courteously.

"She's alright. She manages her arthritis better now. My sisters are married off quite well too."

"I know, I got the invitations. Well, what about your marriage? Aren't you ready for it yet?"

"All in good time, sir. Right now, I am busy building my career. I keep working to better my Kathakali troupe, teaching and guiding students both from India and abroad."

"You must be making a lot of money with those '*madammas*' who are ready to pay a sky high fee even for inferior performances. Don't you, young man?"

"I do not exploit the trend, sir. I try to give them value for their money; I always give them the real deal. Therefore, there's no dearth of students at my institute."

"Shalini was crazy about Kathakali as a kid, I remember. You could go watch some of the live performances there, don't you think?" her uncle put in. He was gently prodding her to giving up her resistance, as he imagined it was, in opening up to Chandran.

"And now, Chandran. Do me a favour. Whenever you have the time, do escort Shalini around the place when she is on her jaunts. I would feel more safe for her if I know that a person like you is there to help her find her way around."

"With pleasure, sir. I shall see that she meets with no harm."

"She seems to be getting bored sitting at home already. It would be a great help if you could show her the interesting places in and around this place. I am too old for that sort of a job now."

"Don't you worry, sir. I shall take good care of your niece and show her the most interesting sights of this place that is native to me."

Chandran was actually being asked to do them a favour! He assured them of taking good care of her.

"But be careful to keep a courteous distance in your friendship. People can talk, you know."

The timely reminder made him reply hastily, "Rest assured, sir. I know my limits in a relationship."

Shalini pretended to be offended that her uncle was insisting on an 'escort' for her. "I am quite capable of finding my way around. Why should you want somebody assisting me?"

"You may be smart enough to get around, as you may remember places you frequented during your childhood, but it sets my mind at rest to know that there is somebody with you who knows the place better. I shall brook no argument on this."

Chandran pretended to be hesitant at first too, but soon seemed to agree with her uncle's advice. "I have some work pending here, but since you so desire, I shall postpone it and take madam around."

"That's settled then. Bring her back before dark, or at least make a phone call if you happen to be getting late." He gave Chandran his phone number, just in case.

'I'll go and change." Shalini tried not to appear too eager. She changed into a light blue churidar with a black salwar and a matching scarf. As she had come from Delhi, her relatives had come to accept her liberal dressing style without much protest.

They were off in a few minutes, with her uncle's 'blessings'. As Chandran had already planned before, they made their way to the city which was a few kilometres away.

Chapter 9

Happy Times

Unlike in Delhi, they had to keep their distance in the bus. Seats were 'reserved' for women here. They alighted after about half an hour at the main bus stop near town. They then took an auto to the nearest beach, which was Baby beach near St. Angelo's fort. After exploring the Fort a bit, they went down to spend some time at the beach. They watched the sunset and soon enough, it was time to head back. Shalini told Chandran that she was not interested in visiting places of historical importance anymore. She just wanted to have some fun with him, spend a few precious moments with him. Thus, they decided not to visit the popular tourist spots, but to roam in and around their homesteads the next day onwards. They reached her home a little after sunset and Chandran assured her uncle that they would come back earlier from the next day. He explained that it was their visit to the beach to watch the sunset that had delayed them. Though hesitant at first, her uncle eventually accepted their explanation.

The trip had provided moments of extreme pleasure to Shalini, like when they raced along the shore of the beach, got all drenched in water and fell on top of each other, laughing in sheer joy. They had to dry themselves while watching the colourful sunset. For some of those moments, they had felt like rollicking teenagers. Shalini had watched in delight as the 'serious' Kathakali dancer became a young boy again, lapping up her praise and wonder.

"We'll do this again, dear, by the river near my home. We shall try swimming there too. Today I was not prepared for it." They had already had a cup of tea at a wayside eatery and were munching on roasted groundnuts from cone shaped paper cups being sold on the beach. The sound of the gentle waves had always had a calming effect on her mind.

"What's your plan for tomorrow, dear? I have only two days left before I leave, Chandru."

"I have made plans. I'll share them with you tomorrow itself."

Chandran's penchant for fuelling her suspense had not left him. He had a twinkle in his eyes.

"We can't afford to be later than we already are today, Shalu. Or, the curtains would fall on all our plans from tomorrow. Let's hurry up." As it was a public place, he did not indulge in any outward gestures of passion, though she was yearning for some such sign. They hurried back and she had to be content with just holding his hand.

The next day, Chandran arrived early in the morning. He informed the uncle that he planned to take her to the temple up a hill near the river. She got ready in time, as he had informed her before of the approximate time of his arrival. She had on a sari that morning, but he asked her to change into a more practical churidar dress, as it would be better for climbing and trekking. He also informed her aunt that they would eat lunch at some place on the way, waving aside all her objections. He had a bag slung over his shoulders with some essentials like water bottles and such.

After a kilometre of walking, they had to make an ascent towards the temple uphill. Chandran, she noticed, was agility personified. He did not seem to be getting tired at all, whereas she felt breathless each time the climb became too steep. It must be due his hard training as a Kathakali performer, she figured. He waited patiently for her to catch up and gave her a hand at places to help her out, especially at one point where she slipped over a hard steep surface. Once they reached the top of the hill, she took a deep breath. The view in front of them was breath-taking. The ascent had been completely worth it. Chandran put his arms round her and drew her close, pointing out the distant river and appreciating the scenic beauty around them. She saw the little cluster of villages at a distance, between the winding river and the distant mountains. Over the slopes of the different hills, she saw how the local farmers cultivated rubber from the rows and rows of rubber trees grown in systematic plantations. Rubber and paddy cultivation was the mainstay of the farmers of that locality.

"What do you say, Shaḷu, when you thus behold the enchanting beauty of such a place?"

"I am speechless. I never realised that there was such a place tucked away in this locality."

There were rocks jutting out of the uneven ground amidst the wild grass atop the hill, where one could perch, albeit precariously. The temple was nearby. When they entered the temple, the priest was just finishing with the *pooja* for the day. Chandran had to take off his shirt before entering the temple. All over Kerala, people can enter temples only if they are dressed according to the temple's regulations. Men have to take off their shirts and don dhotis. Chandran had brought one specially for the purpose. In bigger temples, women in churidars were not allowed, Shalini knew. Since this one was a less frequented temple, the priest did not raise an objection to her entering in a churidar. There were no other devotees besides the two of them there. After their prayers and perambulations around the deity, they gave the *Poojary* (priest) his *dakshina* (an offering of money) and got the *prasad* from him in return. They walked away from the precincts of the temple. After appreciating the view around for one last time, and breathing in the fresh cool air on the hilltop, they started their downward climb. Chandran had looked really handsome shirtless while at the temple, his muscles and broad shoulders tapering down to a narrow waist glistening in the sun, clad in just a dhoti, as was the custom. He looked even more endearing as he carefully guided her down the descent. She tripped over loose rocks a couple of times, but he was always at her side unfailingly, lending the support of his strong arms. The long and arduous *Kalari* training had come to his aid at a time like this.

"We could try and go for a boating trip, Shalu. Let me enquire about the possibility."

They started walking towards the river they had seen from the top of the hill. None of the few passers-by recognised Shalini, as it had been years since she last came down to that place. She relished every moment of their togetherness. She clung to him, opening herself up to him even better. She was impressed by his little acts of kindness towards the people he knew, his courtesy and extreme concern for the elderly and his thoughtfulness towards her. He bought small token presents for her from wayside shops, which she found very touching. In his own familiar neighbourhood, he seemed to have grown in stature.

Shalini understood that he was greatly respected in his neighbourhood, as a great Kathakali maestro, as a persevering man who had climbed the ladder of success on his own, as one who inspired youngsters to work their way up, despite all hurdles in life. He was always ready to help the needy, and even sponsored struggling artists like he had been himself in his earlier days. He was never the one to shirk duties and the responsibilities he had with regard to his mother and siblings, and the various well-wishers. Shalini gathered all this by his talks and interactions with other people on the way. She expected the same commitment and loyalty from him in his relations with her, as she had seen him extending towards the others.

As for him, Chandran considered himself to be the luckiest man alive. His dream girl, that too from a family he had never hoped to even be considered equal to, was walking by his side, in his hometown, and in such close intimacy. He liked and respected her for her dignified bearing, her grace and beauty, at times her child-like innocence too, despite her high education. He loved pointing out hitherto unnoticed things about his native place to her. She had never travelled to this part of his hometown before, being the 'protected' female of her upper class community. He enjoyed her physical presence, loved talking to her about himself, his past life, as well as his future plans with her. He wished to take her to meet his mother after explaining everything to her. He knew his mother might have difficulty in accepting Shalini, but he was determined to try his best to convince her of his choice, with a reassurance that there would be no problem regarding the match with her people. Both of them, thus lost in their thoughts concerning each other, soon neared the river bank which they had seen from afar.

There was no proper dock (boat jetty) there. There were a few local '*vanchis*' or small open boats anchored here and there with the respective boatmen ready to ferry people across the river. Chandran hailed one of these men and asked him to lend one of those boats to them in exchange for a fixed sum of money. He wanted ferry the boat himself. After some haggling about the price, one man let them use his decorative boat which was kept apart for tourists.

Shalini gingerly stepped into the boat, helped by Chandran, and they were off with Chandran gently plying the boat. Like in any other task that he took upon himself, he proved to be an expert at handling the boat too. His capable arms gently guided the boat over the calm waters of the river. The sight of Chandran rowing the boat through the calm river, against the backdrop of distant mountains and the stretch of water behind them, was an unforgettable one for Shalini.

She reflected that she would treasure these moments for ever. Chandran started humming aloud the lines from a once popular Hindi movie, "Mera pyar be tu hai , ye bahar be tu hai…"

To this, she uncertainly added, "Tu he nazaron se aaye tamanna, tu he nazaron me. Um.. hm uh um.."

This was also one of her favourite Hindi film songs. The glittering waters flowing by, the distant sight of the mountains, hills and the valley through which the river went winding up into the horizon as she imagined, with Chandran at the helm of the boat, this scenic beauty was going to be treasured forever in her mind. What more could she want in life? That her life would thus flow endlessly into eternity with her beloved by her side, she imagined. She suddenly became aware of her surroundings as Chandran pointed out the sights on either side of the river. This river was mainly used for commercial purposes to transport wooden logs as merchandise to be sold at various whole–sale depots elsewhere, he explained. It was yet to develop into a tourist hotspot.

After taking a few rounds up and down, not far from the bank where the boat had originally been tethered, they came back. There had been a few anxious moments when the boat bobbed up and down and rocked to and fro at some spots, which had scared her into thinking that their boat would flip and sink due to the undercurrents. Not that they did not know how to swim, but the unpleasantness of getting drenched with the river water would have spoilt half the fun of their outing. She used to wonder why film heroines were always getting drenched, perhaps to increase their sexual allure. If there had indeed been undercurrents, she later reflected, they would have been borne far out into the waters. Anyhow, nothing went amiss during their trip. She sent up a silent prayer in gratitude for it. These were happy times for Shalini. The memories of this outing with Chandran promised to be etched forever in her mind.

It was almost time for lunch. Chandran took her through a different path this time. There was a wayside restaurant nearby, from where they had a good local meal. After generously tipping the waiter, who was surprised at the amount, as receiving a tip from a local was unheard of there, they walked back to a path less frequented by passers-by.

"This is safer," he told her.

"I'm taking you to meet my folks at home, Shalu. My place is very close by, just about a kilometre from here." There was an evident sense of pride in his voice as he spoke of his home and people.

"Alright, if you feel it is really safe." She could not keep the sarcasm out of her assent. He chose to ignore it.

Chandran guided her through a different path. After a few turns, they came upon a clearing that was landscaped beautifully. Shalini had been expecting a typical small house with a tiled roof, but to her pleasant surprise, his house was a decently large two storey'd building. It had a grand entrance that served as a portico, with a car shed attached on one side. It had quite fittingly been named, *'Chandravilasam'*. The modernity of the marble and concrete structure bespoke his sound financial backing. The pillars supporting the corners of the car shed were made out of granite. A few steps lead to the living area within.

He lead her in to a comfortable space, furnished with a reclining sofa and a settee made up of two single seaters and one three-seater. They were arranged around a teakwood panel supporting the T.V. set. As they entered, a woman in her late fifties greeted Chandran.

"Aarannu Chandra koode?"

The local slang was slightly difficult to follow for Shalini, but she translated it roughly to herself so as to figure out who it was.

"Ente Amme, evirenekku Delhiyil vechu ariyunnavarannu." He explained to his mother about his acquaintance with her in Delhi.

"Berin, irikkin. Oru kappi edukatta?" Her generous hospitality was evident in her offer of a cup of coffee. However, Shalini politely declined.

Chandran's mother was a dark, short statured woman with an engaging smile. It was her sharp features and smile that Chandran had inherited. She stood observing Shalini and seemed to like her. She was wearing an off-white *'settu mundu,'* the traditional Kerala attire, which seemed a bit soiled, suggesting that she had perhaps come straight from the kitchen. On hearing the sounds in the hall, Chandran's sister came out to enquire too. She had a kid in her arms, whose wailing she was unsuccessfully trying to stop. She was also attired in a *'mundu'* and *'veshti'*. A comely woman, she was dark like her brother.

"Edunna berunne? Naadu eede aanoo?" she asked. From where do you come? Is this your native place?

Shalini gathered as much. The local dialect was unusual for her. She had picked up a few words as a child, but they were soon forgotten. Her father had traces of it in his vocabulary too, but her mother had the chaste accent of *'Valluvanadu'*, the literal language more common to them. She had taken after her mother. Chandran's accent was polished, spoken in almost literal Malayalam, perhaps because of his years away from his native place.

Lucky for them, Chandran's family had not recognised her immediately. Chandan had decided to explain everything to them later, by gently breaking it to them. There was bound to be a disagreement of some manner, but Chandran was confident of winning them over.

Chandran's mother had not shown any signs of recognition. Long back, she had come to help out at the main household quite a few times. She would definitely have thrown a fit if she knew her dear son was gallivanting with one of the respectable high-born maidens of the locality. For now, she remained just an acquaintance of Chandran in their eyes. Shalini guessed that he must have brought many such acquaintances to his house in the past, for his mother to not be surprised at this new friend, whom he was showing around. After an exchange of pleasantries which she managed quite well, Shalini got up to depart. It was time for her to go back. She promised to drop in and visit them again some other time. Chandran accompanied her through the gate to the path beyond, from where, with his guidance, she could find her way back to the big house on her own.

"You seem to have made a favourable first impression on them, Shalu," Chandran said, approving of her manners at the meeting.

"You try talking to them, Chandru, and get their approval at the earliest," she reiterated.

"I hope to do just so, my dear. At the earliest too. I am staying here for another fifteen days. I have some unfinished business here. I am planning to buy a few acres of land, a rubber estate to be precise, so as to start some business in rubber. It is a thriving business opportunity at present. We must have something to fall back on when we retire, don't you think so?"

Well, he was planning quite far ahead, thought Shalini. That was a good sign.

"We'll meet at the same place, the *aalthara,* tomorrow at noon and chalk out our future plans, Shalu. It is too risky to talk over the land-line." Shalini nodded in agreement.

As she walked back home, she glanced back to see Chandran waving good-bye at her. The deep yearning and love in him was reflected in his eyes, which she reciprocated likewise. This put her mind at rest, though she had started to have some serious misgivings.

Chapter 10

Parting Pangs

She reached her uncle's house, her temporary home, a little after teatime.

"I had a good time, uncle. We went to the temple up the hill, and then went boating in a '*thoni*'. Chandran is good with a rowboat. It was thoroughly enjoyable."

Her uncle was glad that she had appreciated her outing, though her aunt did not look too pleased.

"Suppose someone had recognised you? I would have had a lot to explain to the plain village folks."

"No one recognised me, dear aunty. Only a few knew Chandran, and they must have thought that I was just some tourist he had brought over."

"Anyway, we have some visits to make to our relatives and neighbours. Come with me." With these words, her aunt walked off. Shalini had but to obey. They first went to the nearby places. The next morning, they were to visit some places, accompanied by her uncle.

The womenfolk in the neighbourhood that they visited were all invariably surprised that Shalini was still single and studying in Delhi. They were essentially simplistic and conservative in their outlook. An unmarried girl over nineteen years of age was beyond their comprehension. Getting married and settling down was the only aim in life for them. Educating a girl beyond the basic 'school final' was deemed unnecessary, even harmful. Shalini sent up a silent prayer of gratitude that her own parents were more progressive in this aspect.

Shalini observed something she was not used to at home with her parents. The women, irrespective of the differences in caste, were so respectful of their menfolk that they were careful of always walking a step or two behind their men. They took a back seat by choice in whatever position they found themselves in or regarding whatever decision they had to make in their lives. There was a definite preference for and bias towards boys, who were meted out special treatment.

The women had willingly internalized the idea of male superiority in every action that involved the males. In her own community, it went to such ridiculous lengths that "Even a seventy-year old woman should get up and show respect to a seven-year old boy," as an old granny had informed her. 'What if the said woman was too weak to get up, or bedridden?' Shalini thought, tongue-in-cheek. That was the age-old dictum followed by the women of her community in these parts. They were in awe of their menfolk. Domestic violence was accepted, even supported, by a majority of women in all communities here, who had made peace with silently suffering any injustice meted out to them. Women were marginalised. Men were mollycoddled even to the age of fifty, and Shalini, with her liberal ideas of equality, felt disgusted. She thanked her stars that Chandran, having gained due exposure of the world outside because of his stay in the metropolitan Delhi, was more liberal in his attitude. Would she have had a similar fate as these pathetic women otherwise? She hurriedly waved such foreboding thoughts away. 'Perhaps, in years to come, the patriarchal attitude of the people here will change and become more progressive,' Shalini hoped.

Shalini was careful to not express these thoughts in front of her aunt and uncle. Having lived there all their lives, they could never understand her. Her aunt considered her uncle '*Pati*

Parmeshwar', catering to all his whims, and they had boys who, in all probability, took after their father too. Her aunt had made her uncle so dependent on her that he couldn't be away from her for even a short length of time - a traditional, devious, but accepted way of bypassing the control of men. Shalini admired the capacity of such conventional women, but preferred a more direct means of influencing men herself.

Shalini came back to the present with a jolt. She had let her thoughts stray too far during the visit to their relatives. They had now reached the main house. The evening sun had gone down, and her aunt got busy lighting the lamp, a daily ritual in the household. It was only after her prayers in the *pooja* room every evening that her aunt went about her dinner preparation. Shalini offered to help, but she gently declined. After an early dinner, she curled up with a book in her bead, as she was not used to sleeping so early. She had only one day left before she went back to her parents.

The next day, after an early breakfast, her aunt and uncle took her to meet some distant relatives. It soon became clear to her that they were showing her off. They proudly presented their niece, the highly educated girl from Delhi. Perhaps at the back of their minds was a wish for a good proposal from a similarly educated eligible young man from within their community. Shalini tried her best to avoid getting involved in such 'match–making' traps of her own people. These people were so simple that they did not understand that these efforts did not go down well with her. She wanted to get back from there as soon as possible.

They returned by noon. After lunch, when her aunt and uncle retired for their afternoon siesta, she quietly slipped out for her meeting with Chandran. He was ready and waiting at the place where they always met. They took a slow walk through the woods nearby.

"Chandru, I have to be back by teatime. I slipped out unnoticed."

"Oh dear, I had expected to spend some more time with you. Alright, let's not waste our time in mere chit chat then."

"Have you told your mother about us, Chandran? What was her reaction?" Her anxious query brought forth the desired response.

"Oh, yes. She was dumbstruck at first and found it hard to believe. But on explaining everything, she finally seemed to come around. She is not entirely comfortable with me aspiring to settle with a high-born person like you. She feels that marriages should be made between social equals for the relationship to be comfortable. Naturally, she wonders how your parents would take it. And she is unhappy about our decision of keeping the affair a secret, till we register a civil marriage. She had wanted my marriage to be a grand affair, conducted right here in our native place."

Shalini felt relieved. One major hurdle was past. Though she did feel guilty about not having informed her parents in advance, she knew that it was better for both of them to be discreet about this for the time being. Her parents might not readily fall in with her line of thought, she knew, especially her mother.

"We'll get busy with the preparations for our marriage as soon as I arrive back in Delhi. We shall first go house hunting, and then shop for essentials to set up a home. That will keep us busy till we can register our marriage."

Chandran's planning regarding their immediate future was meticulous. He seemed to have definite plans regarding the type of house they were going to inhabit, which preferred locality was the best, depending on its affordability. He was definitely more practical. He, therefore, seemed more serious about all this. Shalini had only a vague idea of these things. She was happy to have left these details to him.

He seemed to be planning everything in a hurry. "Take things a bit slow, Chandran. Do not go overboard, do one thing at a time. First try to come to Delhi at the earliest. Then we'll get enthusiastic about all this," Shalini cautioned him.

For some time, they walked in companionable silence, each lost in one's own thoughts of a rosy future. Her heart grew heavy at the thought of separation, albeit temporary, from him. A glance at Chandran's face made her realise that he was finding it quite difficult too. Grief was writ large over his sensitive face. He was putting in a great effort to appear indifferent to the impending parting. In an attempt to laugh it away, an enchanting smile lit up his face.

"I can't wait to get to you there, Shalu. I shall be counting the days."

With these words, he dragged her into a cosy shade and clasped her to himself, as if he would never let her go. She came out of the passionate embrace breathless, but happy and excited.

"I shall eagerly await your presence too, Chandru." There were tears in her eyes; tears of joy at his love, and of sorrow for the forced separation. He was holding onto her hand tightly.

"Will you come to see me off at the station, dear? The train starts at 11.30 A.M. tomorrow."

"I'll try my best, my pet. I'll make it to the station somehow. Goodbye, for now." He suddenly let go off her hands and turned around.

With these words still ringing in her ears, they reached the turning that led to her uncle's house. He walked away without a backward glance and disappeared from her view. Perhaps, he did not want to appear too sentimental.

As she entered the house through the portico, she noticed the presence of some guests inside. Her aunt was speaking in a loud voice to an elderly man and his wife. As she entered the living room, her aunt pointed her out to the old gentleman.

"Oh, this is our Shalu*kutty*? She was such a tiny tot when we last saw her a long time ago. She's grown up into such a beautiful girl," the woman started the conversation.

"Oh, she was so mischievous back then. I remember, she once fell into an ash pit at the back of the main house and got her feet slightly burnt." This bit of information was provided by the gentleman.

Vague memories of those times came back to her. She recalled how she had to go about with a bandaged foot for many days, confined to the side lines of all games, not being able to play with her cousins for nearly two weeks.

"Don't you remember Vasuettan and Amminiedathy, your paternal cousins, Shalini? They were frequent visitors here then," her aunt tried to help her remember.

Shalini nodded politely in assent. She remembered this uncle who had encouraged their drama club when she had been a little girl.

"Have you completed your studies? Do you not think of settling down now?" The conversation invariably veered to the question of her marriage. She was starting to feel uncomfortable. Just then, her uncle interrupted the conversation and the talk turned to sundry matters. She excused herself and escaped into the seclusion and quiet of her room. Shalini was starting to get irritated at the mere mention of marriage, especially when she was trying to deal with the impending absence of Chandran for the next few days. She pretended not to hear when her aunt asked her to come out and see those relatives off. Later, after getting a grip on herself, she came out and offered to help her aunt in preparing dinner. To this, her aunt declined, saying, "Do go now, girl. I know you have the packing to finish for tomorrow. I want to express our heartfelt gratitude to you for having spent all these days here with us. We had never expected that you would ever choose to spend your few days of vacation here. Your uncle is also grateful for your decision to come here. You lit up our days which were getting repetitive and boring."

This was a big speech for her usually reticent aunt. They dearly missed their own children. Her uncle presented her with a new set of clothes – a brand new saree with a matching blouse piece. This was known as *'Onapudava'*, usually gifted to relatives by the oldest member of a family, when they came to visit for the first time. Likewise, they were showing their appreciation of her presence there. She went back to her room after thanking them for everything. She started to pack her things up for her journey the next day.

She sat with them for dinner and accepted with gratitude a bag full of ripe mangoes and some mango pickle, which they gave her as a parting present.

"Your father also likes this pickle and these mangoes, Shalini. Those are for your family. Do remember to write to us. You are always welcome here. Try to come again sometime."

It was touching how they doted on her. Perhaps, since they had no girl child of their own, Shalini was special for them. She bid them goodnight and retired to bed early.

The next morning, she got up early and walked about in the garden with her cup of tea. Along with her sips of tea, she breathed in the cool country air and watched the sun rise at a distance. She had come to love this countryside and was sure to miss it.

"I'll come back, I promise. Once I wed Chandran, I will definitely return as a young bride with stars in my eyes," she whispered to herself. She then went inside to dress up and had breakfast with her aunt and uncle. Her aunt had thoughtfully packed a generous lunch for her. Her uncle drove her to the station. They reached by about 10 o'clock and she boarded the train by eleven. She looked around anxiously for Chandran. As she did not want her uncle to confront him, she requested her uncle to not wait for the train to start.

"It is a long drive back, uncle. Don't bother to wait. The departure may even get delayed. You should start your drive back." Her uncle did feel tired, she could sense, as he said, "You do not mind if I go, dear? I have informed your father of the arrival time. He'll come to pick you up."

"Oh no, uncle. Thanks so much for dropping me. Please pay my regards to aunty."

As she saw her uncle walk away and recede into the distance, she resumed her search for Chandran. Wouldn't he come? Would he fail her this time? A minute later, she caught sight of him hurrying up to her compartment. He seemed breathless. Her face lighted up on seeing him.

"I thought you'd never reach in time!" whispered Shalini. He held on to her hands that she had extended out the window of the train.

"How could I not have come, dear Shalu. I was hiding in the crowd, waiting for your uncle to move off. Listen Shalu, do write to me when you get back. We may not be able to have private conversations on my land-line for too long."

"The same goes for you too, Chandran. I cannot have my parents get suspicious about lengthy phone calls."

They gazed at each other quietly, tongue tied for the moment, oblivious to all the commotion around them at the station. Finally, Chandran found his voice, "I am so glad you could come down and spend a few days with me here at my native place, Shalu. I am also grateful that you agreed to meet my mother, whose approval is important for me, to cement our relationship."

"I'll never forget these days, Chandru. Thank you for escorting me around and caring for me with such love." She was squeezing his hands, not wanting to let go. He was responding in kind, his heart in his eyes, overflowing with affection.

The guard blew his whistle, and the green flag, signalling the departure of the train, got raised. The train started to move slowly, departing exactly on time. Chandran kept walking at the side of her compartment. He kept waving goodbye to her, which she unfailingly reciprocated. He seemed to say, "See you at Delhi, bye." Tears filled her eyes, as she waved back. The train gathered speed as it moved out of the platform. She strained her eyes and neck to see him clearly, but it became possible as the train caught up speed, leaving him and the station behind. Finally, he shrunk to a speck at a distance, which soon faded from view as well.

Shalini sat back with a heavy heart. For a long time after, she sat with her eyes closed, going over the joyful moments she had spent with Chandran over those past few days. The sorrow in her heart made her less appreciative of the usual sights outside the window of the speeding train. She bought a magazine and tried to pass her time reading it, but her thoughts repeatedly wandered back to Chandran and the happy times they had had, both in Delhi and back at his hometown. She could not have enough of them.

Finally, she got a grip on her emotions and started to enjoy her journey. It was a little after dusk that she reached her hometown. Her father was waiting to receive her at the station. The short drive back home was pleasant. Her mother was relieved to see her back. The next few days were uneventful, except for the training in traditional south Indian cooking from her mother, which mostly ended in a disaster. Her father and brother were greatly amused by her efforts, though they tried to cheer her up. She was, however, successful in teaching her mother some north Indian recipes.

The day before her departure for Delhi, some two weeks later, she got a late-night phone call from Chandran. After an exchange of pleasantries and endearments, she informed him of her journey back to Delhi. She gave him the phone number of a friend who stayed close to her place of residence, so that he could call her when he landed back in Delhi. He also told her to not call at his house back in his hometown, but to write him letters, or to wait till he got back to Delhi. As soon as they finished their talk over the phone, bidding goodbyes, her mother entered her room.

"Whom were you talking to, dear? That too, at this time of night," her ever-vigilant mother wanted to know.

"Oh, it was a friend from Delhi, mother. I was telling her I would start back tomorrow and would reach there by the day after. I just want her to keep things ready for me as I stay close to her apartment."

Her mother seemed satisfied by her explanation. She was relieved that there was somebody there to take care of her daughter's needs while she was away. She was always worried about this.

The next day soon dawned. Shalini had packed everything for the journey, including the extra packets of typical Kerala food items provided by her parents. The luggage had grown enormously, but since it was a train journey, she did not mind the additional luggage. Her father and brother went to drop her at the station. Shalini knew that all three of them were upset at her departure. She herself found it difficult to keep back her tears.

"I shall come back for a much longer holiday, mother, once I am awarded with the PhD and get a job," she consoled her mother. Her mother, on the other hand, did not seem too convinced of this.

"Phone us as soon as you get there. Keep in contact," her father reminded her, as she seated herself inside the train. She nodded in assent and waved goodbye to both of them. She was lucky to be put up with a very friendly elderly couple during her journey, who were also bound for Delhi. She was even offered food which she shared with them. They were travelling to their son's place who was employed in Delhi. When they found out that she was travelling alone, they expressed their concern for her.

Chapter 11

Feet of Clay

Her train reached the Delhi station on time. She took an auto to her place of residence, as she was familiar with the route, after bidding goodbye to the elderly couple and thanking them for all their care and concern. She soon joined the course that she had applied for, while awaiting the results of her PhD Viva which was conducted a month later. A month passed, yet there was no news from Chandran. She had written him two urgent letters, to which he had not replied. She had started to get worried. There was still no news from him. Was he being held up by legal formalities? She enquired about him at the institute once or twice, but they had no news from him either, except for a telegraphic message regarding an extension of leave for another two months. Her viva was to be conducted in less than two months and he was not present there to lend her the moral support, though she was aware that the viva was nothing more than a mere formality. He was not present at the proud moment when she was finally awarded her PhD a month later. How she had wanted to share it with him! She informed her parents about her being awarded her PhD. Her father, who knew that she was doing the supplementary course, hastened her in her effort to apply for a lecturer's job either in Delhi, or at her own hometown, after she completed her course.

Almost three months passed after her arrival back in Delhi. She had stopped visiting his Institute by this time. She once chanced upon a foreign student whom she recognised as a member of the institute. She casually asked him, with a heart beating anxiously, "Has your Chandran *Asaan* (teacher) arrived and resumed classes at your institute yet?"

"Yes, ma'am. He arrived last week and has started his classes."

"Oh, I was not aware."

She had difficulty admitting it, for at least some of these long term students were aware of her admiration and fondness for their master. As she walked away from this student, her mind was up in turmoil. He had arrived a week back. Why, in God's name, had he not contacted her? Something was terribly amiss. She had to confront him and find out, face to face, what had gone wrong.

The next day, she took leave from her classes and went straight to the institute. After announcing herself, she rushed on blindly into the director's cabin. Her unexpected and sudden entry made Chandran jump up from his seat, surprising him into a shocking posture.

"What's this, Chandru? Why did you not contact me after you arrived? I demand an explanation." Her words came out in a confused tumble.

He evaded her eyes and replied formally, "How do you do, Shalini? Do take a seat. We have to talk some things over."

She observed that he had addressed her as 'Shalini' and not Shalu.

"What is all this formality for, Chandran? Why did you not contact me on arrival? I waited so long for some news from you. I have eagerly been waiting for you. What about our future plans?"

Chandran had an intensely pained expression on his face. He also looked very tired. He seemed to be trying hard to master the emotions within him. He swallowed once or twice before he spoke, "Shalini, please bear with me. The situation has completely changed since our last meeting. I'll try to explain. Do try to understand and forgive me, if possible."

Shalini could not take his words in. What was he trying to make her understand? What had happened in this gap of a few months for him to appear so distant and formal? She sat down trembling and fearful. Yet, she willed herself to hear him out, knowing full well that it would not be pleasant news.

"Shalini, please listen to what I have to say, with patience. Do you remember what I told you about a maternal cousin of mine? The one who was marked out for me in my younger days as my '*murapennu*', the one I was supposed to marry later on? Tired of waiting for me, and also because I could not look upon her as a wife, she got married to another young man just last year. The week before I was supposed to board the train back to Delhi, a telegram arrived that her husband had died all of a sudden in an accident. I had to go to perform his death rites. When I returned, she accompanied me back to my uncle's home. She was not interested in returning back to the house of her in-laws anymore. She was inconsolable, totally broken due to the tragedy. She had had no children from this marriage, as yet. I had to stay back and give some moral support to my maternal uncle, so I cancelled my ticket to Delhi and extended my leave. My mother also came there to lend support to her only brother and his wife. The sight of their young widowed daughter was heart breaking for her ageing parents."

Shalini wondered what was coming next. Something dreadful, she was sure. Chandran's voice started faltering when he saw her distraught face.

"I know, I shouldn't have delayed coming back. I did not contact you as I didn't want to burden you with my family problems. After the hearing of the legal case I told you about a few days later, I started packing again to come back. I went to meet my uncle one last time to pay my respects, and also to meet and bid goodbye to my mother who had been staying with him. My mother had already told him of my wish to marry you.

"When I met him, he dropped a bombshell on me while giving me his blessings. He said that he knew of my affair with you, but hoped that I would not shirk from my duty towards them. As I stood wondering, he pathetically fell at my feet and cried out, "Do save my daughter, Chandra. See how cruel her fate has been. She has been widowed at such a young age. Please give her another chance at life. Please take her with you as your wedded mate." My mother seemed to be in total agreement with him.

"I stood there as though I had turned to stone. My hopes or my aspirations did not matter to them at all. My mother had raised me and my siblings with great difficulty since the death of my father. Now, at the grief-stricken condition of her only brother, she demanded her pound of flesh from me. She called upon my sense of duty and obligation towards her. She wanted me to save her brother's daughter's life, by marrying her.

"How could I have wriggled out of this difficult situation? I hoped that the said girl, my cousin, would not agree to this conspiracy. But, no. That was not to be. She was only too willing to concede to their plans. I have told you that she had feelings for me when we were growing up. It was because I had discouraged her that she unwillingly married the other guy. I was trapped. My uncle gave me a lecture on how a person should sacrifice his personal desires for the sake of duty. Shalini, O dear girl, I was thus forced against my will to get married to this cousin of mine within a few days! Everybody at home conspired against me in this matter. I had no say in whatever happened and it all went down so suddenly. How could I have informed you of this tragedy in our life? I was not sure how you would react. So I postponed talking you about this, or even contacting you. How could I have faced you? I will never be able to convincingly explain these matters to you, nor convey my utter helplessness in this."

She gazed at him in utter disbelief and helplessness. She covered her bowed head with her hands, struggling to overcome the tears that threatened to gush out. Regardless, he continued, "That my mother and sister at home supported my uncle in this matter, was impossible for me to believe. They urged me on to not abandon this girl. They rode roughshod over my desires and hopes for a future with you. Oh, what was I to do? On one side was the girl I loved, one who trusted me, and on the other side, my duty towards all those who had made me what I am today, especially my mother who even worked as a helper in your house to bring me up. Could I have taken the path of the modern day selfish and self-centred person and let go of my past to live a life with you? Was I to do what we see in films and stories? I couldn't, my love." He paused; there was plain anguish in his voice, which was now breaking.

"I could not choose personal happiness, when my near and dear ones were clearly pained by my decision. I finally made the excruciating but practical decision of sacrificing my love life for a life of, what they reminded me was, my prime duty. How could I ever have conveyed this painful matter to you, or even communicated this to you over phone or a letter? I was waiting to tell this to you directly, but I had to gather sufficient courage to face you first." He looked at her pathetically, imploringly.

She was stunned and speechless at this shocking revelation. Chandran would never guess the deep anguish he had caused her. He called it his duty. Some duty, which did not recognise the heart ache he had caused her, his sincere lover. She sat there unseeing, as he continued, "I fully understand what a great sacrifice it was for you to have disregarded societal norms and customs when you decided to have a love affair with me. But is it not a good thing that your parents and the people from your community do not have an inkling of what transpired between us? Now they need never know about our unhappy affair. You can carry on as if it never happened. Please excuse me, forgive me for what has happened. I do not deserve the likes of you. We can remain simple acquaintances. I have brought my wife, Suma, here. She lives with me now at a place nearby. The relationship we share may not be a romantic one, but is based on the values of fidelity and duty. Once more, I express my deepest guilt and sorrow at the inconvenience that I have caused you, Madam."

He had slipped into formally addressing her as 'madam', which clearly spelt the end of their fairytale relationship. It revealed the formality and distance that he wanted to maintain with her henceforth. She had nothing to say to him, her dignified silence and scornful look spoke volumes. She got up and made an abrupt exit.

Back at her lodgings, she reflected on what he had said. How could he have been so callous? Her uncharted flight, as she had metaphorically imagined their affair, had crash landed, but with mentally bruised survivors. She was the one more shattered and emotionally bruised. He had made a better deal of the unexpected and unhappy event by contracting a marriage.

She could not bear the sorrow. She felt as if her heart would break. For this to have happened after all their planning for a joint future! She had put him on a pedestal, idolised him, while he turned out to be basically a coward, a man with feet of clay. Instead of standing up for her and proclaiming his loyalty for their bond, he had succumbed to his mother's and uncle's persuasions. She had misjudged him. She should have taken a hint when he was able to distance himself so easily from her after his stage performances. Had she confused him with the heroic characters he had portrayed on stage? Had he been inspired so by his characters, that he had successfully play-acted a hero in real life towards her, his real life heroine? She would never know the truth. Now, she was only thankful that he had not exploited their relationship, and had not gone 'all the way' with her. Like he had said, she would have to make a herculean effort to put all this behind her. It had to be a clean break, she tried to think practically with her chaotic mind. She would have to leave Delhi and go back to her hometown. She could not even imagine living so close to the person who had betrayed her trust so completely and had committed the unthinkable.

Soon after, she completed her course and informed her parents of her decision to move back with them. They were overjoyed and eagerly awaited her return.

Chapter 12

On the Rebound

Shalini recalled her life after the great upheaval. She had tried to analyse what had gone wrong with their relationship which made Chandran spring such an unpleasant surprise on her. Without even a warning, too. During her train journey back, she tried to find a hundred excuses for Chandran to have taken such a decision. Perhaps his mother did not really like their relationship, and at the first opportunity that presented itself, she prevailed upon her son to fulfil his duty towards their family. Chandran might have been compromised. So, he chose to give up his love life for the interests of his family members. She could not believe that he could have been so weak in his resolve to be united with her. He belonged to the old guard, she now realised, those who considered duty or dharma above everything else in life. Sacrificing his own desires came easily to him, but she was more sensitive. She kept regretting what a wonderful life they might have had. Actually, in her frenzied mind, she could find no real or logical explanation for Chandran's sudden turn, considering the intensity of the love that they had had for each other before. Perhaps, she had imagined it all. Now she had to overcome her sorrow, be practical and move past this event in her life. With great effort, she tried and succeeded in hiding her grief from her parents and other well-wishers.

She returned to the warm and welcoming home of her parents. Though her parents tried their best to entertain her by taking her to local festivals and performance oriented theatre arts, she often found herself pushed unexpectedly into depression. Her parents wondered why she got up and walked out in the middle of a Kathakali performance once. How could she explain to them that it was a far cry from the actual histrionic performances of Chandran, and that she could not bear to watch such performances by anyone besides him. These plays seemed to be like substandard ones put up by the cultural centres for the benefit of ignorant tourists visiting there. She went along to humour her parents. Though she occasionally came across a good performance by renowned local artists.

The first thing she did was to put in some applications for a lecturer's job at the private colleges nearby. She was lucky to land a job at a prestigious private college there. She was good at managing both a career and a private life at home. Life got busy, what with all her preparations for college, her classroom sessions where she enjoyed interacting with the bright students of the batch, and in developing relations with the other staff members. She became quite popular among the students too. They made it a point to not miss her classes, which were both informative and entertaining. This led to a few ego clashes within the department, but the head of her department whole-heartedly supported her endeavours. She also took the initiative to train her students in various art forms. This lead to them winning laurels for the college in competitive performances. She had no time to brood over her past anymore. Slowly, the influence of these activities in her hometown started to impinge upon her mind. Besides her teaching, she started to cultivate her hobbies again and resumed taking music classes, reading, and engaging in social activities to help the less privileged students who came to her college. Time is the greatest healer, she realised. Within a few months, the memories of her life in Delhi receded to the background of her mind. She had more important things to do in life, and she began looking forward to the different avenues that life was throwing at her to explore.

Almost eight to ten months after she had arrived, she understood that her parents were on the look-out for a 'suitable boy' within her community for her to marry. Though she shied away at the thought of an arranged marriage, she later came around to agree to the idea, after her father gave her the permission to meet and assess the guy for a period of time before saying yes. Her father also promised her that they would drop the case if she found the person too wanting. There weren't too many educated eligible boys within her community, so they had to narrow their search down to two or three young men.

The first was a doctor who had recently completed his internship and was preparing for his PG course in medicine. He seemed impressed that Shalini was a PhD in her subject. However, he and his father wanted to know whether she ranked first in her degree and post-graduation batch, as the 'eligible' doctor had been a rank holder all his life. Both Shalini and her father were put off by their pompousness, especially that of his father. What had they been looking for in a future bride? The best genes? An appropriate gene pool? Highly amused, Shalini was quick to show them to the door. She could bet that they would have demanded a hefty dowry for the 'much favoured groom'.

The next bachelor aspiring for marriage turned out to be a professional banker. A young man, he seemed to be always calculating his next move in life with regard to money. The match definitely promised a pre-planned life, one where they would never want for finances, but Shalini's adventurous nature spurned such a predictable life.

The third person was a man from the armed forces. Quite good-looking, this man, but he was always on the move. Shalini had opted for a settled life back home. She was not comfortable with the idea of frequent transfers, and she did not relish the idea of staying back to just look after her in-laws either, while the lord of the house was busy travelling.

The list quickly thinned down to a last candidate. Her mother voiced her concern at her high handedness and arrogance, as she called it, in turning down such good offers. Her father was more patient with her.

Shalini wondered whether her decision to get married and settle down was a defiant gesture against Chandran's rejection. Was it an act of rebound? Did she genuinely want marriage with some other guy? She had even considered not marrying at all, and to live out her life like a spinster, or even to commit suicide when she could not get the man of her dreams, like some eighteenth or nineteenth century heroine, whose only option was to end her life when she faced such a rejection. On the other hand, her practical self asserted even more strongly. Why should she miss out on the pleasures of her life, like having a family, just because the first person of her choice had denied her the opportunity? He did not deserve her, she thought with a strong sense of self–respect. Whatever reasons he might have had to abandon her, she would not be a coward. She had succeeded in not letting her parents know of her heartbreak. She did not now want to break their hearts by taking a negative stance, while they went ahead with their plans to get her married. Why disappoint them? After all, like Chandran, she also had a duty towards her ageing parents. Why fight them over this matter? She chose, rather, to give in gracefully. Her personal desires had already been sacrificed, she thought, why not then live her life henceforth according to the expectations of her parents and her society? She was sure that they would always have her best interests in their hearts. According to traditional Hindu culture too, sacrifice was the best way of life. She had to completely sacrifice the thoughts of her love life (one that was lost already) to fulfil her duties towards her parents and the society. Why should she be cheated of a chance at a normal life with family and kids, plus a promising career, for the sake of a gutless person and whatever the reason he had given for his turn of situation? She had come to know the extremes of a romantic relationship, the highs and the lows, in her failed love affair. It had ended tragically for her. She had decided that instead of taking a coward's way out, either by sacrificing her personal ambitions of becoming a wife and a mother, or taking her own life out of desperation, she would prove to herself that she could survived her personal tragedy. She owed it to herself in order to boost her confidence in life.

She decided that henceforth, she would live out her life courageously, as her practical nature whispered to her. She would prove to be a survivor by walking into a marriage that promised to be good for her. When an opportunity would present itself in the form of a reasonably good marriage proposal, she would consciously take it and work towards making her marriage a success. She would be really lucky if she did get some positive outcome from taking such an important decision in her life. She kept her hands crossed and prayed fervently for such an event in her life to present itself in future. She had the confidence that she would be able to effectively and efficiently manage her home as well as her career, with a little help from her future spouse. She had already decided that she would never even consider a proposal where the man would not allow her to go to work outside her home.

Chapter 13
Marriage Blues

It was with some trepidation that Shalini agreed to meet her fourth 'suitor'. He was an engineer by profession, working as a civil engineer in one of the big construction companies in her hometown. His name was Sandeep Krishnan, son of one Mr. Krishnan. They belonged to central Kerala; their *tharavad,* or ancestral house, near the main city. So much of information was obtained from their first visit. He had come with his elder brother and his father to 'see' the prospective girl. He was not bad looking himself. He was almost six feet in height, and had a fit and toned body. He was not too fair and was clean shaven, much to Shalini's surprise, unlike the other three, who had sported big and small, even handle-bar moustaches, very typical of the men from Kerala. He was different, perhaps due to his educational sojourn outside Kerala. Shalini was impressed to know that a major part of his education had been from outside the state, which, she hoped to have made him more broadminded. They were allowed to talk to each other, as was the tradition. They were, thus, able to have a private conversation, where they were able to assess each other a little bit. He was open to meeting with her again soon. He seemed to have been impressed with her from the very beginning.

In a few days, both of them were to see each other on a holiday at a nearby hotel. This time, they were able to open up better and more freely. She informed him of her higher studies in Delhi and her work regarding her PhD. He enlightened her with the nature of his training for his professional course at Bangalore. He had completed his B.Tech from an IIT and got an additional M.Tech degree from an institute in Bangalore, before landing the job at the construction company here in her hometown. Much to the delight of his parents, he was nearer to them in Kerala now. His parents stayed with his elder brother in central Kerala. They were well off, financially. Shalini found him to be an engaging young man and a good conversationalist with a biting sense of humour. A few meetings later, as sanctioned by her father, she found herself ready to tie the knot with Sandeep. They informed their respective parents about it, and the date of their marriage was fixed.

When she reflected upon this whirlwind courtship ending in marriage, she knew that she had not fared badly at all. There surely were no tumultuous ups and downs of her former passionate affair with Chandran, but this was a more mature relationship, complete with the blessings of their parents and near and dear ones, as also the full sanction of their society. Perhaps, they could make a success of it, if they could both work with patience on their mutual liking and bonding. She was determined to try her best, as she was sure that Sandeep would too. He was a gentleman. He was patient and gentle with her, polished in his manners. She figured that she would have to control her impulsiveness and wild streak to live up to his good qualities.

Their wedding was a modest affair, yet some called it grand. She met again her uncle and aunt, and their kids from the North, all of whom were very happy for her. After their wedding in her hometown, they went to the house of her in-laws for a day or two. They then returned back to her hometown. Sandeep had taken up a house on rent which was equidistant from her college as well as his construction company. It was only a few kilometres from her parents' house too. She started travelling to her college in her college bus, which came to pick her up at a stop nearby. Sandeep had a small car that took him to his workplace everyday. Many a times, he was picked up by an office car too. Shalini returned back from work by about five, while Sandeep returned back by either six or seven. Shalini also visited her parents every other day, and lent her services to them whenever needed. To say the least, Shalini felt like a contented person after marriage. She grew to love and respect her husband who gave her no cause for complaint. He had no complaints on the home front either. In fact, he admired her ability to combine career management with the managing of their house. In whatever manner he could, he helped her out with the different chores at home. He even proved to be a good cook at times. He was very helpful, gentle and accommodative with her parents as well. They were ever so fond of their son-in-law. Shalini felt very grateful.

Whenever they had an extended leave from work, they went down to visit his parents, who had also come to like and love Shalini. She had good relations with her in-laws. Her elder sister-in-law might have been a wee bit envious of her at first, but grudgingly accepted her soon after, especially when she was given a few presents by Shalini. She was a housewife. They lived in a spacious house. Sandeep's brother had a young son. Shalini, being so fond of kids, soon had the little boy eating out of her hands. This also contributed to lessen the resentment that the boy's mother may have had for Shalini. Sandeep was happy that his new wife had got into the good books of his parents so quickly. They did not resent her going for work. In fact, they encouraged it and were even proud of the fact. In this, they differed significantly from the other people of their community. Elderly women in most families discouraged their daughters-in-law from taking up jobs outside, unless there were financial constraints within the family. Shalini considered herself lucky that her in-laws had no objection to her working, just like her husband.

So as not to start a relationship based on secrets and lies, she had tried to open up to Sandeep about her previous affair, on the very first night after their wedding, but he had hushed her, saying, "No, dear, I do not want to know anything about the life you've had till now. I have also had indiscretions and infatuations while I was studying. Let's look upon them as a lack of maturity of our younger selves. Henceforth, we shall promise to stay committed and true to each other. That is all we need. It is useless to probe into our past if it does nothing to help us build a future. It would only make us unduly suspicious of each other. So, let bygones be bygones."

This mature and generous attitude of her husband won over her trust. Shalini took to heart his advice on this matter. She was relieved that he had not tried to check or question her past. She resolved to be loyal and truthful from that day on in her relationship with her husband and to try to make a success of her marriage. Letting go of her past, however, was easier said than done. She often lapsed into moods of 'what might have been'. At such instances, she had to shake herself out of these ruminations with conscious deliberation. She engaged herself in work, which was a great antidote. Her husband sensed such fluctuations in her moods and helped her by taking her out often to dinner or other means of entertainment, like films. He was no ardent Kathakali fan, but whenever she felt the urge to go and see a performance, he was always ready to accompany her. Slowly, these trips to watch Kathakali performances lessened, till they finally petered out. They kept their social engagements to a minimum, especially within their community. Both of them were in agreement that their folks, the so called well-meaning relatives and friends, were quite narrow minded and interfering. There had been a few incidents which put her off the members of her community, especially the female members.

Three years later, her brother, who had got employment in a distant city, got married to a girl of his choice, albeit from the same community. This match was approved of by her parents, who gave him and his wife their blessings. They had a girl child first and later a boy.

Chapter 14

Settling Down

She was able to observe well the hypocritical behaviour of the people of her community, when they gathered together for parties and weddings. Some of them she observed at their homes, when she visited them with her husband. There was the case of a woman who had had a reasonably good education, but brought up her son and daughter very differently, under the influence of a traditional preference towards the male members of the family. This woman was unable to resist the temptation of giving preference to her idiotic son over her brighter daughter, who was always better at studies and in her behaviour than her brother. The unlucky daughter was always side-lined and belittled. Finally, when she grew up, the daughter found love and consideration in a highly educated man, an outsider, and eloped with him, much to the discomfort of her parents. They were unable to live down this scandal in their society. The parents eventually cut off all relations with her.

There was also the case of uneducated women in their community who spread terrible rumours about women who were educated and went out for jobs. These women conveniently forgot that they availed generous loans from the very same kind of women they had thus cast slurs on. Shalini knew she could not generalise, as there were exceptions to this way of behaviour too, but such meanness in manners was more common among her folk.

Then there were some women who tried to outsmart their rivals at home. All the heavy work would be done by the sincere slogging ones, but once the job was complete, these over-smart ones hogged the credit for all the work by acting efficient in front of the visitors. There were also the women who befriended others only for the various benefits they could reap from such relationships. They were actually jealous of the more educated, tried blindly to imitate their actions, but ending up looking ridiculous. Shalini had a real contempt for such behaviour in those women. While she understood that this behaviour mainly stemmed from a lack of education and choices in their lives, she hated how they hurt other women and found imaginary faults in them all the time, for having outshined them in their efforts.

Some men of the community were partly to blame too. They seemed to support such activities among their women. The higher and nobler they were in the hierarchy within their community, the greater was their bigotry and narrow mindedness. Their inflated male egos and the conventional belief that women were inferior to them, lead to a sorry plight of the women in the community. It was a sort of 'divide and rule' policy. Women could never see the plight of other women sympathetically. They only learnt to mistrust other women and treat them as rivals. They tried to win over their men by the traditional 'weapons' of tears, and sympathy fishing. No woman dared to assert herself openly for the fear of being branded arrogant, unruly and unwomanly. They had to 'save face' in front of others. So, they put on their best behaviour whenever there was an audience. Shalini knew a female relation who put up an elaborate 'show' of grief in front of her visiting relatives on the death of her mother-in-law whom she hated and treated badly, for as long as she was alive and well. Only those who could act well could survive gracefully and win accolades in such a vicious atmosphere. Shalini knew she could never be a successful 'actor' in such circumstances. She studiously avoided the company of such women. She also avoided the company of the so called 'ideal wives' who blindly catered to all the unreasonable wishes of their husbands. There were some men who ordered their wives to fetch to them everything, right from a glass of water to a pen, even when these very things were well within their reach. Were these lords and masters of the house so handicapped, that they could not rise up and get such a simple work done by themselves, without the help of their wives? Many women did it out of the fear of their spouses' angry reactions, Shalini observed. Such male chauvinism! This was, in part, encouraged by the women themselves, who took pride in proclaiming, "My man can do nothing without me. He is a disaster in the kitchen, so I tell him not to enter such places." What an escape this was from the boring household chores for these genetically lazy men of her community!

Many boys from this community of hers either refused to take up higher studies, or were not qualified for it, being sons of a lineage of landlords. They abhorred physical work and were never inclined to put in any effort to better themselves, despite being sufficiently qualified. Some of them ended up as priests in nearby temples. The moneyed among them set up some small businesses of their own, which usually ended as failed ventures. Most of the less educated men with low IQs stayed with their parents as dependents, pretending to be ideal sons who preferred to 'looking after' their parents, than to have good, independent careers themselves. No wonder, some of the older men and women who supported them were so selfish and self–centred themselves that they stood in the way of the upliftment of their own sons in their chosen careers, if it demanded being separated from them. Such male progeny who sacrificed their ambitions for the sake of their parents, were highly appreciated. As time passed, however, such lesser qualified men began to find it difficult to get compatible brides in marriage, as girls became increasingly better qualified and did not mind rejecting the proposals of marriage from such worthless men.

Shalini observed that whatever achievements or education a girl acquired, it was side lined, belittled, and looked down upon by most people within her community. Rare indeed were people who encouraged the female child to go forward in her education and conquer heights, to win name and fame in her field of choice. To 'get married, be a good wife, bring up good children, look after the elders, your husband, home and kids' should be her only motto in life, was the only advice handed out to women. It was high time that such egoistic, high-handed, traditional men and women who blindly supported this ideal, were reformed, Shalini hoped. All of this was done in the name of family relations, to maintain the 'status quo'. There were men who treated women as totally insignificant, lifelong burdens, making them emotionally so dependent on them, that they became blind to the fact that the men were exploiting them left, right and centre. They actually made the women suffer for their own insecurities, as they were inadequate themselves to deal with their problems in life. The women who suffered as a result, were so well trained in hiding their real feelings, that they spoke in defence of such men and belittled the women who transgressed the unwritten rules. At the other end of the spectrum, however, were also those women who had managed to make their men utterly dependent on them, so much that such men became mere 'putty' in their hands. There were men in their community who thought nothing of abandoning their duly wedded wives of long years, and strike up relationships with other attractive women. Marital fidelity was at a low premium for such men. Women in such situations were always supposed to 'grin and bear with it'; the 'boys will be boys' refrain.

Shalini thanked God that her husband was the faithful kind, who showed due respect to all the womenfolk, including her, and was much more liberal in his attitude towards the rights of women. He had never given her a cause for complaint, and had adjusted so well to her many needs that had arisen due to the pressure she underwent when she combined managing her career with taking care of their house, her husband and her child. She had earned the respect of her parents-in-law for the way she coped with all of it. She felt blessed for this.

This inequality was especially prevalent in the joint families of old. The co-wives and sisters-in-law were always at each other's throats. Simple things like sharing food often became a bone of contention, and erupted into major quarrels. They did not know the basic fact that for a joint family to survive in those harrowing times, there needed be a lot of sharing, and give and take between the members of the families living under the same roof. It was not limited just to the sharing of finances, which was done out of convenience. Selfishness in even one member was enough to disrupt the peace of a family. The women tended to blame each other after carrying tales about one another to sympathetic listeners. The older generation found fault with the younger generation. In such situations, there should always be a strong, diplomatic, but compassionate head of the family who could manage all these members in conflict, thought Shalini when she came to know of some such families. Otherwise, many a times, the spineless men who support vile women in such critical moments, add fuel to fire. This leads, in most cases, to the younger members moving out of the joint family to the comparative peacefulness of a nuclear set up. It took some time for Shalini to observe and understand the undercurrents and personal politics within her community, and finally accept and adjust to them while settling down in her own new life. She was grateful to God that she did not have to undergo such humiliating experiences in her husband's home. Shalini wondered if the people in her community would ever get over such retrogressive attitudes when it came to giving due worth to the efforts of women, and considering them as equals in competent fields of activity where they had proven their worth.

Chapter 15
Joys of A Wife And Mother

Sandeep was good as a sexual partner. He gently initiated her into a satisfactory partnership in bed. After some time, it did become a bit repetitive and predictable, but he never tired of surprising her at times. She was able to experience the heights of physical passion due to his careful handling of sex. Though the emotional and physical frenzy she had experienced with Chandran was missing in this saner relationship, she was happy and content with just this. He cared for her enough to keep her happy in their relationship, both physically and emotionally. She had no time to brood over her unfortunate past unnecessarily. They had settled into a comfortable relationship. At times, Shalini's rebellious nature broke out in arguments on issues she held dear, but Sandeep was almost always able to bring her around to understand his point of view, though he had no ego hassles. When time permitted and when they had sufficient leave from their respective jobs, they took off to holiday destinations. Both of them enjoyed such relaxing trips. They were yet to go on long journeys, or to foreign locations, but Sandeep promised her that he would try and take her on foreign trips sometime in future.

In about two years, their joy was compounded by the birth of an adorable child, a son. They named their son Vijay, to symbolise their successful go at marriage. Shalini's days became hectic, as she got occupied with looking after the kid, going through the daily chores, catering to her husband and managing preparations for her job as well. They had to cancel many of their vacation trips till the child was older. Her parents helped her in looking after the baby till he was old enough to go to school, and even afterwards.

After the baby was born, both of them adjusted their outings by taking the baby along with them. He became the centre of their existence, their joy and pleasure. Shalini's relations with her in–laws became even better. The grandparents doted on their grandson, showering him with presents whenever they visited. Whenever Shalini's parents were unable to take care of the child, her in–laws gladly took over the responsibility. The child was quite a handful, naughty and vigorous all the time. So much so, that Shalini and Sandeep mutually decided not to have another child after him. Both of them were busy with their careers too. His brother had a baby girl a year after Vijay was born. Shalini's time was taken up by the daily chores and looking after the needs of the growing baby. She had no time to ruminate over her past mistakes.

Her mornings grew hectic. She had to get up early to prepare food for herself and her husband. They used to take home cooked food for lunch to their respective workplaces. Before leaving for college, she also had to take the child to her parents' place. They would look after the child till she returned from work in the evening. This was so much better than leaving the child at a crèche. The child also got the benefit of being looked after by his own grandparents. Shalini considered it her good luck that she had her parents living nearby. They made much of their adorable grandchild. The child was also quite attached to his grandparents. They put up with all his stubbornness and naughtiness.

Every moment with the child was precious for Shalini. The day its first tooth sprouted, the day he took his first steps, were special landmarks during his growing years. She had loved his toothless grin as much as she loved his smile made up of those tiny sprouting teeth. How he had run around on all fours, slowly learning to get around on his chubby wobbly feet! They took snaps and preserved these memories in an album.

His first words, 'momm' and 'dda' were music to her ears. She tried to teach him words in his mother tongue. They were easy words, but he lisped along at first, without clarity. Slowly, he started picking up the easier words. Sandeep also helped her in this, each evening after coming home from his office. The boy used to rush out at the sound of his father's car easing into the driveway. After having his tea, the father made it a point to play with and entertain his toddler. When Shalini was busy in the kitchen, Sandeep often took him out on short walks. He would be carried on his shoulders initially, but once he learnt to walk well, his father made him walk alongside him for some time, holding onto his hands and guiding him. Both would come back home rejuvenated. They would try telling stories from illustrated comic books to him. His grandparents, when they were looking after him, fed him with stories from the Puranas, especially the exploits of Sri Krishna as a young child. It became difficult to control him when he started imitating the mischievous behaviour of Krishna at home, like climbing up the stairs or the balcony to pick up or topple items out of his reach, imagining them to be vessels filled with milk or butter. They all had to keep a vigilant eye on him. Sometimes, after having been quite naughty and infuriating his parents, he would go into hiding to escape slight punishments. After a thorough search, they would come upon him hiding beneath a table or even a rack inside the kitchen shelf. How he managed to squeeze into those places was ever a mystery. His laughing face, gurgling over with innocence and joy, was always enough to melt her anger. He would get swept up into her arms and kissed, ever so affectionately.

He loved playing in a tub of water, a true water baby. When she had to take a bath, she kept him by her side in a wide tub of water. He shouted lustily when he played in the water, splashing it all around him. There were times when she felt too exhausted having to put up with his pranks after coming home from work. Her husband, however, helped her as best as he could in managing the boy. He was usually not very destructive, but developed a temper on certain occasions, which required a disciplined handling. At such times, her husband managed him better than Shalini could. She understood that the boy had a resolute nature which enabled him to get around both his parents and grandparents in acquiring whatever he had set his mind on. The main problem was that there were no children of his age nearby with whom he could strike up a friendship and play outdoors. All his play was thus confined to the adult companionship of his parents and grandparents, within the four walls of their houses. Shalini knew that this was not healthy for a boy growing up. He mouthed dialogues far beyond his young years while conversing with his parents, criticising them like his grandparents did. She thought that perhaps starting to go to school would help him outgrow his dependence on his grandparents and parents. He was also becoming addicted to children's programmes on T.V., a habit which they wanted to bring down.

When Vijay started school, he was reluctant at first, but soon mingled with the kids there and obtained many friends. He went to school in a school bus, which also brought him back after his classes. He was bright for his age, but he was hyperactive and restless at times. Shalini was told that this was because he was more intelligent than many others in his class. So, she had to keep him active and indulged even after he returned from school. She enrolled him in a music and painting classes, since he showed a penchant for these arts. This was during weekends. On all other days, her husband engaged him in games and took him out for walks at times. There were a few other families whose school-going children soon joined Vijay in his games in an open play ground nearby. They would come to pick him up from home, and bring him back after their sporting activities. Now, after his evening bath and studies, he got very little time left for T.V., which came as a big relief for Shalini. He turned in soon after nine o'clock every evening, putting in a healthy eight to nine hours of sleep. Both parents were relieved. Reports from his school, when they took turns to attend the PTA meetings, were also encouraging. He made good grades in his class, being one of the toppers. They never insisted or pushed him to come out the first in his class.

Vijay acquired a taste and skill for music as he grew older. Shalini introduced him to the nuances of Kathakali music. He accompanied her to watch some performances too. She found that he was not too interested in the Kathakali performances, though he appreciated them regardless. He liked the music more. As he grew up, he came to understand his mother's love for the art more than his father's. But gradually, he was weaned from the influence of the music of his countryside. He grew more interested in Hollywood music, especially the peppy numbers. When he grew up even further, he got hooked onto the jazzy western numbers and rock music of the west. Shalini could not digest the so called western music, which always sounded too loud to her, but she tried to be enthusiastic about the romantic and melodious songs. After all, music was not supposed to have any barriers, if one could enjoy it. Her husband did not even pretend to tolerate the 'blaring noise', as he called it. He was a total traditionalist at heart, when it came to interests in the fine arts.

Chapter 16

Childhood Reminiscences

He loved to visit his paternal house for vacations, where his uncle lived with the grandparents and family. He could then play with his cousins. He seemed to have a liking for rough games at times, but he was caring and protective about his baby cousin sister who they did not take with them when they played outside.

Once, when he was very young, about three years old, and was playing outdoors, Shalini remembered, the boys, her son and his uncle's son, together chanced to go up to the pond nearby. It was their private pond with a bathing ghat, but they had been warned to steer clear of the place. Yet, Vijay's fascination with playing in water drew him along. His older cousin, senior to Vijay by two years, boasted that he could swim very well and jumped into the water. He was soon splashing around. Vijay could not contain his curiosity. He waded into the waters too, which soon closed over him menacingly. At that sight, the older boy panicked. He was not big enough yet to try and rescue his little brother. He rushed out of the water, ran into the house and shouted to the folks inside that his younger brother had disappeared into the water. The men folk ran out and with the help of a male servant, fished the unconscious Vijay out of the waters. He was rushed to a nearby hospital for first aid. Luckily for him, not too much time had elapsed after he went down and before his rescue.

After some water had been pumped out and a resuscitation attempt, he regained consciousness. He was thus 'born again', literally. A shocked Shalini heaved a sigh of relief when she found out that he was out of danger.

This episode made Shalini and her husband more vigilant of their son's outings. Sandeep enrolled him for swimming classes too. He soon became an expert swimmer. After this, whenever he went to his paternal grandparent's home, he would still go swimming with his brother, but always with some adult supervision.

When in primary school, Shalini used to get worried when she checked his schoolbag in the evening and saw that Vijay had brought home bright objects from school. She even found that his pencil box contained colourful pencils which they had not bought for him. Was he stealing from his friends' pencil boxes? Would he grow up to become a common thief? She did not know how to tackle this problem. She shared her anxiety with her husband who promptly, but gently, took him aside and questioned him.

"Whose pencils are these, son?"

"They are from my friend's box."

"Why did you take them? Did he give them to you?"

"No, Dad. I took them when he was not looking and hid them in my bag. They looked so beautiful. He brings a lot of pencils. You give me only one or two."

"Son, never take another person's belongings without the person's permission. Tell me if you want something. I shall buy you whatever is possible. Okay, son? Return all these things back to those kids tomorrow itself."

With this timely advice, Sandeep took his son to a nearby play store, bought him dozens of colourful pencils and a few other attractive items he wanted, and brought him home totally happy and satisfied. Vijay promptly returned all those items that he had borrowed from the other kids who had not even noticed their absence. He never repeated the offence again. In this manner, early in life, the tendency of the child to take possession of things belonging to others, or in baser language, the provocation to steal, was thus nipped in the bud. This was done by the father by a clever but psychological intervention at the right moment. It was from then on that Vijay became a model student. He was able to charm his teachers and other kids his age, some of whom became his lifelong friends.

Leadership qualities became evident in the boy right at the beginning when he was in fourth standard. A particular incident had highlighted it, Shalini remembered it quite well. Vijay had mentioned a boy in their class who used to bully them often. He made the other boys do menial jobs for him like carrying his school bag and his slippers, and liked to walk with a swagger in front of them, like their leader. He would also pick up a fight with whoever disobeyed him. A few days later, it had only been a week since Vijay joined the gang, the big bully asked Vijay to do a menial job for him and Vijay refused to oblige. The boy gave him a slap on his face. Vijay reciprocated angrily by slapping him hard in return. This led to fisticuffs and even wrestling. Despite his small size, Vijay was able to knock out his opponent. The hurt bully rushed to complain to the head teacher, but all the other students who had witnessed the incident supported Vijay. Thus, he became their hero and together they managed to control the bully from pestering other students. That day Shalini realized that whenever needed, Vijay would rise to the occasion, take care of his own self and the others who sincerely stood by him. He was almost always right in whatever cause he stood up for. He was interested in fighting only for what he thought was right.

They had brought him up without any biases of caste differences that was strictly adhered to by the older generation in both Shalini's and Sandeep's families back home. If at all he asked embarrassing questions about it, picked up from his friends at school, they made it a point to tell him that it was an unjust system. As a consequence of their liberal attitude, he brought home many friends belonging to all religions and castes. None, including his grandparents, accorded them any difference in treatment, much to Shalini's relief.

By about seven years of age, Vijay was initiated into the rituals of becoming a proper Brahmin along with his cousin brother, through the ceremony of 'Upanayana' and 'Samavarthana', after which he was supposed to wear a sacred thread around his shoulders, denoting that he belonged to the upper Brahmin caste. He thus became metaphorically 'twice born', once at birth and the second time after this initiation. Shalini remembered how he was 'born again' after he had accidentally drowned himself when he was three years old. The function was held at their *tharavad,* as insisted by his paternal grandparents. He had to walk around with a shaved head with a tuft of hair on the top for a few days. He found this mortifying. He had to don a cap to school for a few days till his hair grew back. The other students had a good laugh when they observed him in an almost 'Yule Brenner' style. His father taught him to bear the insults with dignity and forbearance, however. Though Sandeep and Shalini did not believe in such rituals of initiation, they had agreed to all this for the sake of Vijay's grandparents.

Soon after they returned to their home and workplace, Vijay abandoned the sacred thread. His father did not insist on him to wear it. Sandeep knew that his friends would make fun of him for this too. So they gave him permission to dress the way he wanted and discard the so called sacred thread if he did not want it. Although, they instructed him that as long as his grandparents were there, or whenever he visited them, he should wear a readymade thread over his shoulders so as to avoid unnecessary questioning and probing by his father's relatives. Vijay readily agreed to this arrangement as he was fond of his grandparents and his uncle. He was even ready to visit temples whenever his parents went, or when they insisted.

They took him for short vacations to nearby places like Malampuzha, Ooty, Bangalore, Kodaikanal and other famous places during his vacations. Both Shalini and the boy had vacations at the same time. The boy thoroughly enjoyed such trips. He was quite adventurous, and they always had to be on the lookout that he did not wander off to dangerous places alone. The sheer beauty of these places was not lost on Shalini and her husband, but most of their time was taken up by running after the kid. When he was older, they went on tours to European countries. She liked the British Isles and Switzerland the best. Greece and Venice came a close second for her. She could never forget the gondola ride she had in Venice.

Chapter 17
College Days

Vijay was growing up fast. He cleared his school finals with flying colours. He joined a private college nearby for further studies. He used to take a private bus to and from college. He did not want to join the college where his mother was a lecturer. He knew that the rebellious streak in him made him trouble prone, thus he did not want to embarrass his mother if at all he got into a fix at college. Perhaps due to the attention he got from the fairer sex, Vijay started frequenting the gym and built up his body to almost a six pack, a finely sculpted one. Shalini was proud of the fact that he was tall for his age, a six-footer, with broad shoulders and a narrow waist, which he had inherited from his father. He was also on the fair side. Best of all, however, he was essentially a good person, full of respect for his seniors and the elderly, a trait not very common in boys his age. He was always well mannered and polite, but he was not weak. He stood up for all the righteous causes in college. He was a favourite of all the teachers who supported him when he raised his voice against any perceived injustice. He was fully supportive of the girl students and their problems. Vijay formed a group that took up the genuine problems of students and even fought for them. He was against joining any political group with extreme ideals, though. He was more of a moderate in his political ideals. He was pressurised more than once to join one of the politically oriented groups due to his immense popularity among students, but he refused to bow down to their dictates.

Shalini remembered him as a curious child in his younger days, with so many questions about the life he saw around him. He used to confide in her about most of the happenings at his school. He was always caring and concerned for her well-being. Whenever she was able to, she would try and sort out his problems and advise him on the desired course of action. When she couldn't solve them, she passed them onto her husband who had infinite patience with his child and his queries. As he grew older, however, she observed a certain distancing in his approach towards her. He seemed to have started to confide in her husband more. They were almost like friends. Shalini was so scared that he would fall into bad friendship, or take to drinking, or become a drug addict. She need not have worried on this score, though. Her husband gently guided him in the right direction, though he also had his doubts at a certain point in time.

"Dad, don't you worry. The principles you have taught me have not gone to waste. I always abide by them. I choose my pals very carefully. Though I have been betrayed by a few in the past, I am now careful in choosing my friends. I avoid the super-rich friends who always like to show off. I am aware of our middle-class background. And the hard work that you and mom have put in to get me where I am now. So relax, dad. Whenever such wayward friends compel me to join their sexual escapades, my dear mother's face comes to my mind. I run away from such 'friends'. Do believe me; I have been able to avoid the temptations so far only because of your guidance."

When her husband reported this to her, Shalini felt totally relieved. She had been assailed with doubts and tensions when he first started college, but now they were put to rest. They never indulged him too much or gave him too much pocket money, but just enough for his daily expenses. Therefore, he had not been spoilt. This had helped him to value the importance of money. He never wasted his money unnecessarily. Shalini came to know from certain reliable sources that he lent his money to needy students sometimes. She felt so grateful when she came to know about this, that she willingly increased his pocket money at such times. She did not have to worry about him in any matter. He was an ideal student. He spent all his excess physical energy in sports and body building, and enhanced his mental energy by reading a lot, besides his commitment to studies. She was able to concentrate more on her career because of this.

At the outset of her career, she had found it a struggle to come to terms with her teaching schedule. For her, work had been no less than a therapy to overcome her wounded soul. But she soon found herself quite caught up in her work. She came to love it and its challenges which she took up sincerely and cheerfully. Her classes were popular. Her lectures were attended by most students. Many a times, she even noticed students who came from afar, to throng to her classes and be in time for her lectures. When she inquired these students about it, they answered in one voice, "Ma'am, even if we miss other classes, we do not like to miss your lectures. They are so inspiring!"

She took a personal interest in her students' welfare. In some of her classes, she once observed a few back benchers skipping class. On enquiring about their absence, she found out that they were frequenting some local bars. They had also been seen skipping classes to go to films. She doubted that they might have picked up a habit of using drugs besides drinking. She alerted the principal, who was a strong person. After a meeting with the other staff, they contacted the parents of these children. They were advised to take prompt action to reform their children, or to take them out of their college. This timely intervention by Shalini and the other teachers, including the Principal, saved the lives and careers of at least some of the erring students.

Once, there was the incident of one of her favourite students turning listless, inattentive and sleepy in class. This student had been very attentive in her first year, scoring high marks during the class exams. Shalini wondered what could have happened to her. She asked the student to meet her in the staffroom during recess. When she came to meet her, she refused to answer, looking sullen and cross. She was asked to bring her parents before entering the class again. She brought her mother the next day. On enquiry, Shalini understood that the mother was bringing up the child alone. The father was toiling away in one of the Gulf countries. Of late, the mother told Shalini, her daughter seemed quite distracted and not inclined towards studies, as she had been earlier.

"Madam, could you please give her some coaching classes after her regular classes? She says she likes your classes best. Could you please help her out in whatever she lags behind?"

Shalini did not have the heart to refuse the desperate mother who wanted her only daughter to do well in her education. So, she arranged to help her out after her regular class. The student's mother sent her to Shalini's home at a convenient time. When she came for her extra classes, Shalini tried to find out what had happened to the kid. The student reacted strangely.

"What is the matter, child? Why don't you want to study well? Why don't you do your homework? You were so hardworking and brilliant. Is it some problem at home? Is your mother too strict? Tell me."

"My mother loves me. She is not strict at all."

"Then why don't you listen to her when she asks you to study? Why are you so stubborn? Look here. See if you can read through a page of this text that I have given you and try to answer the questions given below. Your exams are around the corner. Let us see whether you can answer them or not."

Shalini gave her the work as a test and left her for a few minutes. When she came back after some time, the girl was still sitting with the paper, staring at it blankly. She had just scribbled something incomprehensible on the paper.

"What is this, girl? Why are you wasting my time and yours by not doing what I asked you to? I just wanted to check your ability to pick up the correct answers. Otherwise, how do I know what I am supposed to guide you with?"

"But I will not listen to you, Miss. I have a personal guide who tells me what to do. I will listen only to him. Let him tell me what to study. Then I shall do it with all sincerity. I shall not listen to either you or my mother."

Shalini had the shock of her life. What was the matter with this kid? She had been one of the most respectful and obedient students in the past. How had she turned so arrogant and obstinate? And who was this guide she was talking about?

"Who are you talking about, child? Who is this personal guide of yours? When does he give you all these instructions?"

"Oh, he is a great person, ma'am. I meet him many days on my way from college. Do you know the left-hand corner on the main road leading up to our college? There is a cosmetics shop nearby. On some days, when I am late from college on my way home, this man stands there and beckons to me. He wears a long robe over his shirt and pants. When I go to him, he takes me to a restaurant nearby, we have coffee and snacks and he tells me about so many things. He advises me on what I should do with my life, he tells me what to study seriously and even offers to help me out. He is so gentle with me. I shall do only what he tells me to do. I shall take up studies seriously only if he tells me to."

Shalini was still reeling under the shock of her revelation. Was the child a victim of sexual abuse? Had what happened to her made her crazy? She hurriedly suspended her class for the day. She told her to bring the mother the next day.

When the girl brought her mother the next day, Shalini probed the cause of the student's behaviour. The mother was in tears and said, "Madam, this is the real problem with the child. She talks about an instructor who calls out to her from a corner of the street. She claims that he tells her what to do and she obeys him."

"How long has she been showing such behaviour? Has she been sexually exploited by someone?"

"This started about a few months ago. Her father had just come down from the Gulf on a few days leave. She is very fond of her father and hates it when he goes back. She was inconsolable and in tears when he left this time. But he had to go back as it is our bread and butter. A few days after he left, she started slackening in her studies. I noticed her sitting around, staring blankly into space. She became indifferent to food and her dressing. I had to force her to go to college."

"She must have missed the presence of her father a lot."

"She then started having strange dreams at night. She could not sleep well. She used to cry out in her sleep. I slept with her and am witness to her troubled state of mind. After a few days, she seemed to have calmed down. Her sleeplessness came down drastically. But then, she started talking of this person she had met on her way to college. I panicked. I followed her without her knowledge. At the particular corner that she mentioned, I saw her stop. She seemed to shout a welcome to someone. Then she stood there in the corner and started talking to an imaginary person. There was no one there, Miss. I swear. She seemed to be talking to herself. After some time, she seemed to bid goodbye to that person and moved towards the direction of her college. This is what is happening to my child, madam. I tried following her a few other times too. The same thing happened again and again. Sometimes she gets violent if we do not humour her. She firmly believes in that person she claims she is in contact with. I wonder whether she has gone mad. Oh, what am I to do? I would like to see her as normal as she was before all this happened. Some other teachers recommended you to me, as you are known to be good at handling troublesome kids."

Shalini heaved a sigh of relief. She felt good that she had asked the mother to come promptly. What if the unfortunate girl had become violent all of a sudden? Such persons are known to hurt those that they perceive as adversaries.

"I might have solved the problems of some kids before, but the case with your child seems to be deeply psychological. I am no psychology consultant. I can take you to a professional and try and help you solve this case," Shalini said after listening to the girl's story.

"O please, madam, that would be so helpful."

On the next convenient day, she made an appointment with a famous psychologist. She took the mother and daughter to him. After questioning the girl separately, the psychologist took both of them into confidence. He explained that due to some mental trauma, and not sexual exploitation, the girl was suffering from a condition called schizophrenia. The illness could come down, if it was treated with proper medication and counselling for an extended period of time, but it might not be completely cured. The family members had to be patient with her and lend full support. Out of curiosity, Shalini asked him why the girl spoke of an invisible mentor, to which the psychologist explained that this was one of the main symptoms of the disorder. Those affected hallucinate, or create imaginary characters, with whom they carry on conversations. This boosts their mental and physical energies. The patients prefer the company of those imaginary persons, rather than real people - a type of escapism from the harsh realities of their existence.

Shalini left the mother and daughter, with an overwhelming sense of pity and sadness. The student had to leave the college. She later came to know that after an effective treatment of the illness, as it had only been in the initial stages in her mind, the girl joined a correspondence course and completed her degree. Shalini was happy to know that the girl had later married well and moved on in life. What had happened to her earlier was forgotten as a bad dream.

So many such sob stories came her way during her tenure as a lecturer in the college. In whatever small manner she was able to, she brought solace to the victims and their parents. Sometimes, the help extended was financial; sometimes, it was just a timely intervention or guidance. This gave her the reputation of being a generous hearted person, helping other persons in distress. This very fact earned her the envy and mistrust of some of her colleagues. They tried to malign her name, spreading rumours about her relationships with her students. They complained that she was using unconventional methods in teaching to gain cheap popularity, or that she had political ambitions. In fact, she steered clear of politics, both at her workplace and outside. She was only humanitarian in her charitable pursuits.

The students loved and enjoyed her classes. She used to enact relevant scenes from the text to give a visual impact. She used slides to explain things. She encouraged her students to express themselves by conducting debates during free hours. She inspired them to read good books in their spare time. The students became confident under her guidance. She also encouraged them to better their artistic abilities, so that many of them took part in competitions and brought back prizes. She was very fond of the students who sang or showed histrionic abilities. The principal and the head of her department supported her in all these projects, so she did not bother to reciprocate to those who found fault with her, though she was occasionally upset. At home, her husband and her son fully supported her in these activities, in fact, they encouraged her out-of-the-way efforts at teaching. She had the wholehearted appreciation of her enthusiastic students and their parents. She even won the best teacher award instituted by the founder of the institution.

Meanwhile, Vijay completed the basic degree that he needed to get into a professional course. After clearing the entrance exam, he got admission at a reputed engineering college in the same district. The engineering college was at a faraway place, but they had a college bus which took him to and fro, so he became a day scholar at the place. He used to come home tired everyday, but he did not slacken in his studies. He had less time for body building exercises, but he got enough exercise by playing volleyball and tennis at college. His father became vigilant once more, as the parents were anxious that he should not fall into bad company. Sandeep tracked his movements, at times, without his knowledge, but Vijay was always given a clean chit.

One of their neighbour's sons who had joined the course the same time as Vijay, got into a group that did drugs and got drunk. Sandeep was sorry when he came to know about the apparent decline of his friend's son. The boy was soon expelled from the college due to his anti-social activities and unruly behaviour. Vijay soon became popular in the engineering college. He was a regular topper in his class and stood first in instrumental and vocal music too, which he had learnt quite well. His parents were proud of his achievements. He passed the final exams with distinction marks.

"Mom, Dad, I would like to enrol for an MBA at some institute, preferably in north India or outside the country, maybe the U.S. I want to start preparing for that."

Their hopes of Vijay joining a job in their own hometown were dashed, but they were careful not to show their disappointment. Shalini knew of many parents in their community who discouraged their sons from either studying further, or from going to other states or countries for further studies or jobs. They insisted that once the parents grew older, their sons were duty-bound to stay behind and live with them, sacrificing their personal ambitions, and there were many a foolish unambitious sons who did exactly that. Shalini and Sandeep, however, did not belong to such a group. They encouraged his ambitions. Being their only son, Sandeep had wanted him to be near them, at least, in their own state, but he chose to go north, so they tried not to dampen his enthusiasm for the betterment of his career. He soon got an admission in an institute in Delhi, where he wanted to join an MBA course. Shalini later came to know that he actually wanted to take the qualifying exams to go to the USA after completing his MBA and landing a job in a U.S. based company. She felt that he did not share her enthusiasm to work for his own country, when it came to getting a plum job. With a sinking heart, they saw him off at the airport in a plane bound for Delhi, where he was supposed to attend the interview for his admission into the MBA course. 'Love them enough to let them go,' was the saying which they had to reluctantly accept. She was happy that he was going to be in Delhi for the duration of this course. She was familiar with Delhi herself from when she had studied. When he phoned them later to inform that he had got admission at the Delhi Institute, they were both happy for him, but they had to deal with his absence at home, which was a tough job.

Chapter 18

Unexpected Turns

Shalini was better able to deal with her son not being at home, than her husband who was quite distraught initially. She busied herself with her job and other routine tasks, but it was more difficult for her husband who had come to depend on the boy more. He was about to retire in a year. He was diagnosed with diabetes, so he started to go on long walks. He refused to take any medicine and was often indifferent to his health. Though Shalini begged him to take better care of himself, he refused to listen to her and his other well-wishers. If she cautioned him too much, he complained, "You want to turn me into a suffering patient? Why can't I try to be healthy without medicines? I shall diet and exercise carefully, so that my sugar level becomes steady." He never wanted to be called a diabetic patient. His ego did not permit any acknowledgement of weakness in his body.

Sure enough, when the time came for him to take his sugar test, Shalini found that his sugar levels were indeed under control. Much later, she found out that as soon as the test date was fixed, he would diet and exercise so vigorously that his sugar levels always remained steady and less than the limit prescribed. He had thus fooled both her and their doctor, but he had to pay a heavy price for this later. A few months passed and Shalini found out that she was diabetic herself. Unlike her husband, she preferred to take the medicines prescribed by her doctor, so she was able to maintain her sugar levels well. She felt that 'sweetness' had literally gone out of her life when she was asked to restrict her sugar intake. She had loved to consume sweet things so much. Their son was very much concerned about their life–style disease. He phoned them about it all the time after he came to know about the matter, but they asked him not to worry, as they were taking care of it. He also tried to persuade his adamant father to take medication for his condition, but his father refused. Shalini and Sandeep started to go for long walks in the evening during free time, as it was recommended by their doctor.

Sandeep's father suffered a stroke at about this time. Though he was given good medical care and attention by his family members while he was at the hospital, he passed away in a few months. His wife, Sandeep's mother, had been so attached to him that she also passed away within a few months. Vijay had to come down for their death rites. A year after, his maternal grandmother died of cancer, which was found to be at an advanced stage. Shalini had to take a lot of days' leave for her cancer treatment. Her brother's wife also helped out occasionally. She brought her father to stay with her, despite his reluctance to do it. Her father, a traditionalist, believed it to be demeaning to stay permanently with a daughter. Since he could not adjust to his son's workplace, which was quite far away, he had become helpless, so he accepted Shalini's offer to look after him. Due to all these occurrences, her husband started to seem stressed out.

After about a year and a half of their son having left for higher studies, her husband collapsed suddenly one day. It had been just six months since his retirement. He had been complaining that he was fed up of the 'retired life' and hated not having a job to do. He was also a bit irritated by the presence of his old-fashioned father-in-law at home, who tended to philosophise and argue with him over everything. What could Shalini do? She had a few more years to pass before retirement. She asked him to keep himself busy by taking up part time work at a nearby company which hired retired hands. Even that did not give him enough satisfaction. Perhaps these reasons triggered his physical breakdown. With the help of neighbours, Shalini got him admitted to a nearby hospital. The doctors told her that he had suffered a massive heart attack and that he had barely survived. After a correct diagnosis, he was informed that he had to undergo an operation for the removal of a few dangerous blocks in his blood vessels. He had to be kept under observation in the ICU. She informed her son, who took leave and flew down to be near him during this critical period. Despite the best medical care, he passed away in his sleep on the hospital bed, perhaps due to another attack just before the scheduled operation. His brother's family and other close relatives and friends rushed down when they heard about his sudden death.

Shalini had imagined her marriage and a life with her husband to have gone on uninterrupted. This flight had been precisely charted and chartered, with a clear destination, as she had imagined. But as ill luck could have it, this flight had also crash landed, with only her son and herself as survivors. The person whom they had taken for granted, on whom they depended, had left them both forever, so suddenly. She feared being left all alone to survive and move on in life, once her son flew back to Delhi.

Shalini and her son were heart-broken, completely inconsolable initially. Regardless, her son was a great moral support for her, but he left soon after performing the death rites about twelve days later. As it was, he had taken too many days of leave already. Shalini had to let him go. She had her aging father near her, which was a great moral support. The old man was also hurt and grieving for his son-in-law, whom he had respected and loved in his own way. The doctors told her that a lack of a busy and fit occupation after his retirement and his refusal to take medications for his diabetic condition had hastened his end.

Soon, she had to resume her college work. From being a double income'd family, they were reduced to a single income one, after her husband's demise. Her husband had no pension arrangements, as his had been a private company. He had got a lump sum on retirement, which he had invested wisely, but the income from it was to start coming in only after two years. She could not afford to sit back and relax, or take too many days leave. Life slowly started to lead her on forward. She had to move on. The immediate pain receded.

She had to learn many things from scratch. It was difficult for her to handle her husband's money matters and income tax problems, to supervise his affairs back in his hometown, which he had previously managed with his brother, and so many other things which he had never troubled his wife with when he had been alive. She now realized that there was some resistance against her efforts in these matters from his own people, including her brother-in-law. By dint of her willingness to learn and her hard work, besides managing her job and her home, she was able to overcome these hardships and survive in the best possible manner. She earned the respect of her immediate in-laws. There were quite a few unhappy incidents where she was treated almost like an 'untouchable', as she was now a widow, during auspicious occasions like marriages and poojas, by the cousins in her husband's family, as well as in her own ancestral home. She was ostracised by her own in-laws when it came to social get-togethers and other functions. She had to put up with these insults silently. Who was she to call for a change in the unwritten norms of the traditional society? At such times, she blamed her husband for having left her so suddenly, without preparing her for the inevitable consequences. Though at heart, she knew that it had not been his choice to die at such a time.

When she looked back at the momentous events in her life, with all its twists and turns, she had to admit that her married life with her late husband had been the best part for her, and she had nothing to regret about it. Chandran had loved her passionately, but he could not keep the promises he had made to her about having a meaningful life with her. Her husband had married her and kept up the gallant promises of sustaining and nourishing their marriage and commitment throughout. Of the two, she now realised that her husband was the far better man. Like an observation from a recent Bollywood film, where the heroine, who had loved a man earlier, but had gotten married to another later, realises much that, "Pyar karna asaan hai, lekin pyar nibhana, mushkil." The translation goes somewhat thus:

'It is easy to love (as in a passionate love affair), but it is far more difficult to keep and sustain your love (as in an honest marriage).' The heroine of the film chose to stand by her loyal husband, even after the former lover who professed undying love for her, came back to get her. She cherished all those precious moments of love that she had shared with her dear departed. Such is the power of a good marriage. She hoped that her son would also be blessed with a similar lucky marriage.

Shalini found that her initial sympathisers, including her in-laws, had slowly faded from the scene. She had to fend for herself. At every turn, she encountered resistance, but her job gave her a lot of confidence. She found some true friends who stood by her in her times of great need. Her father and son were great moral supports for her to move on in her daily life. Despite all this, there were moments when she longed for the comforting and strong presence of her departed husband. That was never going to happen ever again. She had seen his cold, inert body being lapped up by flames. She finally trained her mind to accept the permanence of his loss with great difficulty. However, she experienced his strong spiritual guidance in everything, even when she faltered or found herself in doubt.

She decided to sell some of his assets from his father's place, as she was not practically able to manage it from her place of work. Her brother-in-law, who believed, like an idiot, that his dead brother's assets rightfully belonged to him, resisted her efforts in this direction. He refused to accept the legal ruling that a dead man's property and other assets really, legally, belonged to his wife and children.

When she went down to inspect her husband's property, her brother-in-law came rushing towards her, shouting at the top of his voice, 'Don't you dare enter these premises. This is our common family property, and you have no right to enter or do anything about it'.

Shalini wondered how his attitude had changed overnight and so drastically since his brother's death. The thought of acquiring his brother's assets by unlawful methods and his avariciousness had made him blind to the legal truth, and so hurtful towards her and her son. She decided that if he created real trouble, she would have to file a case against him. Initially, she was reluctant to take up a case against family members, but she kept it as a last measure. She then informed her son of these new developments, who told her to wait it out for a while. If his uncle became too provocative, he promised to come down and try to deal with the issue himself. They could consult a lawyer and take the right action then.

When her son came down the next time, which was after a gap of three months, both of them went to consult a good lawyer over his uncle's adamant attitude. The lawyer assured them of their decision to take a legal action against the brother, in case of his unnecessary interference. His demands had no legal standing. The lawyer told them to go ahead with the sales if they had the support of legal documents. That was the time that Shalini remembered that the main document was still with the brother. She had only a copy of it. Some of his cousins had advised him to cling on to it for dear life, if he wanted to take over his brother's property. The lawyer, however, gave them confidence in this aspect. If the worst came about and he refused to give the documents for sales purposes, they could serve a legal notice and make him bring it to court. Shalini and her son were relieved at this possibility. For the time being, things were settled. She started looking around for various sale propositions.

Chapter 19

Shocking Revelation

A week before he left for Delhi after his father's death rites, her son suddenly said to her, "Mom, I would like to discuss a personal matter with you."

They were just about to go in for lunch. Shalini wondered what the matter could be, considering the serious tone of her son's voice.

"In the past one year, I have grown close to a female co-student at our MBA course. I had wanted to discuss this matter with Father, but unfortunately, his demise made me put off the talk."

At the widening of Shalini's eyes and shocked expression, he further explained, "Rest assured, Mother. She is a Malayali, but born and brought up in Delhi. She is beautiful and very well behaved, but she does not belong to our community. That, I cannot help. She also reciprocates my feelings wholeheartedly."

It took Shalini some time to register the fact. Was history repeating itself? What would be the final outcome of this affair between her son and that girl?

"Son, do her parents know about this? Would they approve?" This was her first query.

"Do not worry on that account. She has her family's blessings, especially her father's. He knows that I am planning to go abroad. Bhavana also supports me in my decision. She is very intelligent. Both of us, after our final MBA exams, are taking qualifying entrance tests to go to the U.S. We are planning to get married after the completion of our course. I shall try and get a post in an American based company here that might give me an opportunity to go to the U.S."

Shalini heard the news with total disbelief and a sinking heart. He had planned it out so well. There was now no hope of his ever returning to his hometown, ever. She had to survive among the wolves, the ruthless relatives and well-wishers, all alone. She had nursed a fond hope, like any traditional mother, that he would be at her side now that she was widowed and all alone, lending support in her old age, but all such hopes were dashed, once and for all. Of course, he would guide her from afar. Of that, she was sure. It would have made a world of a difference, however, to be supported from right there, rather than from so many miles apart. She kept these thoughts to herself. She did not want to disturb him with the conditions there, especially when he was hopefully looking forward to a future with his chosen girl. She had to love him enough to let him go, she reminded herself once again. She tried to take more interest in her future daughter-in-law. When he seemed so determined, she could not voice a disapproval against his choice.

"Do you have her photo, dear? Just so I can imagine what she looks like."

He readily brought out a snap of the girl, Bhavana. She indeed looked very attractive and intelligent in the photo. She was slightly on the darker side, but with sharp features and a slim figure. An aquiline nose, grey eyes, a beautiful smile and even white teeth. No wonder her son fell for her.

"She's highly accomplished in fine arts also, mom. She is a good *Bharata natyam* dancer. She has learnt South Indian Carnatic music also. She has inherited all these artistic talents from her father. He is now the honorary head of a famous Kathakali Institute based in Delhi. His name is Mr. Chandran Nair, you might have heard of him."

Shalini's heart missed a beat. This was a shock least expected. Was fate playing an ironic game with her? The cruel gods who had denied her a life with her former lover, were now laughing at her, playing with her emotions, wrecking utter havoc with her muddled mind. How could she be sure that, taking after her father, the girl would not dump her son at the last minute too, turning his life into hell? She could not even whisper these thoughts aloud, seeing how obstinate and determined her son was about his affair with the girl and his desire to marry her.

Observing her stricken expression, her son hastened to add, "Do not be upset, Mom. She is a very obedient and adjusting person. I am sure she will be a great daughter-in-law to you."

"Are you sure of her feelings towards you, my son? Has she shown any wavering tendency in her attitude when you discussed with her your plans to go abroad?" Shalini tried to probe gently.

"What do you mean, mother? It was she who encouraged me on it, when I myself did not feel very hopeful about the matter. I even got depressed at times thinking about this. She gave me hope and helps me even now to achieve my goal."

"Does she have a sibling to look after her parents when she goes away?"

"No, mom. She is the only daughter, but it did not stand in the way when she spoke of this to her father. He was ready to let her go with me in all my future plans. Mom, the great news is that her father is from the northern parts of Kerala too. He says he knew my maternal grandparents. They had encouraged him to take up Kathakali as his career."

The revelation was shocking, to say the least. She knew too well that he was encouraged to follow a career in Kathakali by her own family members. Had he told him everything of his past? She hoped not. It would be too embarrassing for her if her past affair with Chandran had been revealed to her son. That might even make her son withdraw his affair and one more girl would inadvertently become the victim of a failed love affair.

"What else did he tell you, son?"

"Nothing more. He seemed regretful that he could never go back to his native place to settle down. He also seemed stunned at first when he heard your name. He sympathised with me, offering me condolences at my father's passing away. He has been a widower for the past three years too. One of his sisters and her son, who is employed at a firm in Delhi, are now staying with him to look after his and his daughter's needs. It was he who pushed me on to discuss this matter with you, mom. He was insistent that you should be informed and that your blessings should be sought for our union."

At least he remembered and respected her enough to make her son get her consent and blessings. She was silently gratified at the thought. He seemed to be sure that she would have no objection to her son taking up with a girl from a lower community.

"Mother, Bhavna was not in favour of becoming intimate with me at first. She was afraid of the consequences within our rigid community. It was I who took the initiative in pursuing her and finally broke apart her objections. I told her that I was the person to decide our fate and future, that my parents would stand by me in whatever decision I took in this regard. I hope you will not fail me in this, mom. I had earlier wanted to reveal this to father, who would have then prepared you mentally to face this. But unfortunately, I did not get the chance to talk it out with him. Please forgive me for not giving you a hint of this before. I know it is too sudden for you to give your approval immediately. But do try to bear with me, mother, and give us your blessings to take this to a satisfactory conclusion."

If only he knew the truth of the matter! It had always been she who had taken the initiative in her affair with Chandran long ago. It was he who had backed out. Being a woman, she had to watch helplessly as her life and dreams with him slipped away, when he gave in to familial pressure. Her son was made of the same steely determination and a strong backbone, which made him stick to his decision, come what may. But she had failed in her pursuit of love because it was Chandran who backed out. She had realised that as a woman, she could not have done anything to save the situation. But in this case, her son, since he was the man here, was able to pull off a successful attempt at their relationship, hopefully leading up to marriage in due course. What happened to her in the past might never be repeated. She sincerely hoped and believed that he would never succumb to external pressures to pull back from this relationship, as long as he truly believed in it. Outwardly, she kept up her anxious questioning.

"Being an only daughter, isn't she likely to be impulsive and spoilt? Would she have the maturity to handle your problems?"

"Don't you start worrying about all this, Mother. You'll realise when you meet her, how capable she is. It was she who advised me when I was indecisive about opting for a life abroad. Even though she was against it, she gave me positive encouragement."

"I do hope she'll support you all along and that she'll not drop you when she gets a better proposal." Shalini couldn't help voicing her inner fear.

"How can you talk such rubbish, mother? Why are you so suspicious of her motives? I would never have chosen her had I felt that she was an opportunist or a flirt. Don't you trust my mature judgement? Her manners are exemplary and she was more concerned about how you would feel about my choosing to go abroad."

She decided to trust the instincts of her son and welcome her future daughter-in-law with open arms.

"Son, I would like to meet her once before you decide to tie the knot."

"Sure, mother. I'll take permission from her father and bring her down here when we get a few days off after our next exams."

That was all she could get him to promise. Soon, he had gone back to Delhi. Shalini's emotions were in a cesspool of confusion. What an utter coincidence it was that her son had fallen in love with the daughter of the very man whom she had initially had the ill luck to fall in love with. Like the Greeks say, the jealous gods had been against their relationship, and destroyed it. Now they chose to play with the emotions of their children. At least, this time, she hoped that these gods would allow their mutual passion to bear fruit and guide their children towards a successful marriage. If all had gone well long ago, Vijay might have been born as Chandran's son. Shalini was overwhelmed at the thought. Perhaps, buried deep in her heart, she still had a soft corner for him, if it was not love. She was not sure. It was a strange play of fate that Vijay chose to love the very person whom she would have wanted him to avoid. If only she had known about this earlier. Now she could do nothing but bow down to the unexpected and ironic moves of fate, and hope for the best outcome.

A few months later, when they obtained a few days' leave before taking their final exams, Vijay came down to Kerala with Bhavana. Shalini's first meeting with the girl was quite moving for her. She was a good match for the impulsive Vijay. Passionate towards Vijay, she appeared quite calm and serene, mature and concerned for both of them, and for her. Shalini came to like her more as she got acquainted with her better. The same quality of gentleness and assertiveness that she had sensed in Chandran long back, was present in her as well. She was sure that in time, she would come to love Bhavana just as her own daughter and not just as a daughter-in-law.

"Mother, don't you worry. Even if we leave for America, it will be only for a few years. I shall try to persuade him to come back to India and we shall live together."

Shalini was glad to hear it. She was pleased to know that the girl had guessed her real worry about Vijay's attitude. She was thankful that Bhavana would at least try and prevail upon her son and encourage him to return to India, even if he left for a foreign country in the near future.

"Keep this in confidence, Mother. If Vijay came to know about this plan of mine now, he would become obstinate and refuse to come back. I have also to think about my ageing father who needs my presence and care more and more."

Shalini understood that she loved her father deeply. She was relieved that the girl was not too selfish, blind to the needs of the ageing parents, her father and Vijay's mother, that was herself. Vijay was surely lucky to have met her and loved her. Shalini was aware that in these modern times, it was difficult to come across such unselfish girls or boys who bothered thus about their old and helpless parents. She thanked God that Vijay had selected a gem of a girl, who was not only beautiful, but also so well mannered. Both of them left after a few days. She wholeheartedly gave them her blessings for all their endeavours. Before leaving, Bhavana invited Shalini to come to Delhi to meet her father at least once before their marriage. Though she protested mildly, Vijay was insistent that she come to Delhi for the purpose. She said that she would think about it.

Days sped by. They cleared their final exams. Vijay applied for a job at an American company, while Bhavana got a job at an India-based company. Preparations for their marriage got started. They had decided for it to take place in Delhi. Vijay wanted a registered marriage. Later, if Bhavana desired, she could opt for a simple Nair wedding, for the benefit of the public. This was also due to the fact that her father found it difficult to travel back to his native place. He had recently suffered a stroke, which had left him unable to travel too much. There was no one there either, his mother having died ten years ago. His other sister stayed with her kids in Bombay. It was his youngest sister and son who were with him. Only the closest family members were to be invited to the wedding. As for Vijay, there was only his widowed mother and his closest uncles, maternal and paternal, and his grandfather, who were ready to attend his wedding. That too, if he sent them, his uncles, a return ticket to Kerala. Soon, all this was agreed upon and settled.

When Shalini broke this news to her father, she was relieved that he had not objected to it, nor created any fuss. He was just glad that his grandson was getting married. He was beyond caring what caste or community Vijay's bride belonged to. He did not remember Chandran Nair at all, who hailed from his own home village. Shalini was thankful about this as she now did not have any explanations to give about Chandran's past.

For the convenience of his aged grandfather, Vijay booked flight tickets for his mother and grandfather, one month in advance. Shalini landed at the Delhi airport with mixed emotions. Vijay had come to receive them. He had taken a flat on rent in a good locality near his office, which he planned to use even after marriage. Shalini liked the spacious flat, though it did not stand in comparison to their house back in their hometown. Her father quickly adapted to a life in the flat too, despite the doubts that she had had about it. After all, it was only for a few days.

Chapter 20

Confessions – Down The Memory Lane

Though she tried postponing it, a meeting with Chandran was unavoidable before the actual date of the wedding. One day, Vijay took her and her father to meet Chandran. He planned to leave them there, go to his job, and then pick them back up in the evening. The prospective bride's father was almost bedridden since the stroke. When she reached the place in Vijay's car, she and her father were taken into his room by the daughter. She was meeting Chandran for the first time after a long gap of so many years. He looked a mere ghost of his former vigorous self. She wondered whether this balding, greying old man with a slight paunch was really the great former artist Chandran. What had she seen in this pathetic old man that made her fall for him all those years ago, she wondered. It must have been the blind infatuation of youth. She could only feel great pity for this gaunt skeletal person who now confronted her. She knew that she looked her age too, but not so weary and beaten perhaps.

As for Chandran, he was seeing his dream goddess for real once more. She had aged gracefully. She was still beautiful in his eyes. He knew that he looked a forlorn sight, with his twisted left arm and a creased face, his inability to sit up and walk without aid. He had a helper to assist him. He spoke words of welcome and hospitality to Shalini's father and to her, and gestured for them to sit on a sofa near his bed. He showed no signs of recognising her, though Shalini understood that he had known her at once, the consummate artist that he was. He spoke with pride of his daughter to her father, sensing that Shalini was keenly listening to whatever he said. She had also, with great difficulty, erased all signs of recognition from her face, after the initial shock of coming face to face with him again.

After the initial pleasantries, her father wanted to rest and was taken to another bedroom. The daughter was busy preparing food in the kitchen. Vijay had left for work, having arranged to pick them up in the evening. The helper was helping the daughter in the kitchen. Thus, she was left alone with Chandran for a few hours or so. For the first two minutes, a tongue-tied silence prevailed when she gazed around the room, before she heard him call her, "Shalu."

These words still had the power to electrify her, she realised. She looked at him. His unfaltering piercing grey eyes, with all their mesmerising effect, were turned upon her yearningly, yet humbly. Her heart was beating fast but she calmed it with a great effort. He had turned to her and with great difficulty and had folded both his arms, which made him seem like he was praying to her.

"Please, Shalu, do not be prejudiced and take it out on my daughter for what I did to you a long time ago. I want her to have a happy married life with her chosen mate. Whatever I have earned in life will be hers in future. What happened to us should not happen to our children, please, I beg of you."

"What do you take me for, an avenging goddess? True, I felt betrayed by you, but that was a long time ago. I also want the best for my son and understand that he is not so chicken-hearted that he would bow down to pressure either from me or anybody else, for that matter, to give up on his commitment towards your daughter."

That silenced him for a while. When he spoke again, it was in a world-weary tone. "I beseech your pardon for the pain I caused you then. Please, please forgive me for my unacceptable behaviour in the past. It was never intentional, nor meant to cause so much pain. I did not have the moral courage to bypass my duties towards my family and accept you then, I admit. My relationship with my wife was merely obligatory. My child became my whole world from the moment she was born. Since the passing away of my wife three years ago, my child is all I have. She had been a good mother to her, though she was simple and rustic. The worlds in the artistic realm that I could not conquer, I want my daughter to acquire. I hope your son will permit her to do this. She is good academically too and has an enviable job now. I am glad that she chose your son to be her soulmate. The relationship that I had wanted with you long ago, I want my daughter to have with your son. My only regret is that your son seems too eager to go abroad, which will lessen my chances of being near her in my condition."

"Your daughter has promised me under strict confidence that she will try to persuade my son to return back to India sometime after they have lived in the U.S. She is very concerned about you. You are very lucky indeed to have such a loving daughter."

She could see his eyes beam with pride for his daughter. "Another thing," she reminded him, "I do not want the children to ever know what had transpired between us during our immature youthful days. It was a foolish indiscretion on my part that I regret now. I would never be able to face my son after such a revelation."

"I know it, dear Shalu. I wish for the same with respect to my daughter. I would never want her to even guess that there might have been something between us. So, let us try to behave as if we are meeting for the first time, but try to be friends rather than just in–laws. I am sure you must have had a happy marriage, judging by how well you have, along with your husband, raised your son. Even I came to love him like the son I never had. I share my condolences for your bereavement. Let's bury our past once and for all."

Shalini wondered how he could appear so composed when she felt so agitated for all her bravado. She stole a glance at him and found that he was also struggling to bring his feelings under control. Just then, his helper came in with a glass of juice for her. He slipped into the role of a friendly host.

"Madam, do have the drink. Lunch will be ready soon. Did you give her father something to drink?" he enquired of his helper.

"Yes, sir. The old man is resting."

As Shalini sat sipping at the drink offered, Chandran launched into one of his speeches about his daughter's artistic pursuits. How easily he had slipped into calling her 'madam' from the endearing 'Shalu' from before. It was an outright change, right in front of her eyes. She also closed her mind tight to any further possibility of bringing up the unfortunate and painful affair from the past that she had experienced with him. They had a satisfying lunch. Shalini was thankful that her future daughter-in-law was also such a good cook. After their lunch, her father wanted to rest further. Her 'would-be' daughter-in-law had to go out to make some purchase, and the helper, after helping Chandran with a visit to the toilet, went out to buy medicines and other supplies. Shalini was left alone with Chandran once again.

He seemed to be in a talkative mood. "Dear Shalu, I wish to inform you that I never forgot the times we had together. They were the only moments I really lived and felt truly alive. The rest of my life was a mere survival to exist. Only my daughter made my life worth living."

"Don't tire yourself, Chandran. What is the use of trying to rake up the past? Neither of us gained anything from it."

"But I must have my say. I cannot let you keep on thinking that I am to be blamed entirely for what happened then. I was forced by my mother to marry her brother's widowed daughter. When I gave life to one woman, it was at the cost of another, the only woman I had ever truly loved. I had to bear the burden of guilt for having sacrificed and destroyed the love we had for each other. I am confessing all this to you to ease the feeling of guilt and terrible sorrow that I had experienced then. Will you please have the heart to forgive me now?"

He lay back silently and closed his eyes for a few minutes. He came back with a renewed vigour. Shalini decided to give him a patient hearing, though she was tight lipped and a little distant for the time being. If only listening would ease his troubled mind, how could she deny him that? That was the least bit of service she could extend to him at that stage. As it was, he was obviously suffering physical pain.

"Dear Shalu, do you remember our trip back to our native place? And before that, our trip to the Taj? I could never forget those journeys. I always wanted to go to Venice with you, the romantic Venice, where we could have had rides on the gondolas."

She did not want to disappoint him by informing that she had already been to Venice with her late husband. Because of the more important issues in her life, these memories had been pushed to the background. He seemed to dwell on them more. She was not one in her later days 'to pine for what is not.' (Shelley)

"Dear Shalu, I can't forget those early days in Delhi when we roamed the streets, just immersed in each other. Our trip to the Taj was quite romantic, as I remember it. Our first physical familiarity with each other. Don't you remember?"

He observed that Shalini had grown red in face. She did not want him to continue in this strain.

"Do not be scared, Shalu, in admitting our feelings from the past. Now I recognise that it was only a stage in our lives. I realise that we have moved beyond all that. I had a different life in reality, and you had yours. We tried to make the best of our given situations. I don't blame you one bit for the life you chose later, and I deserved the life I got. Still, the times I had with you were the best in my life."

"I do agree with you on this point, Chandru. I feel that we have moved beyond the mere physicality of our relationship. It now seems more spiritual, more intellectual. We must have come together even now, to form a bond that could elevate us to a different level, something more lasting." She really believed that her love and concern for him had suffered a sea change, it had metamorphosed into a mature, spiritual sort of love, from the passion ridden feelings of the past. This was also because his fervent appeals for forgiveness and reminding of past incidents left her unmoved. She had distanced herself from the foolish, thoughtless past. She had become mature enough to dismiss all those as mere fantasies of an immature youthful mind. Her real experience of love, which she had had from her dutiful and sincere husband, was far more valuable to her now than her youthful jaunts.

She could see that Chandran was relieved at these words from her. He must have felt that she finally forgave him for having abandoned her all those years ago. He stretched back on his bed, resting. He asked for a glass of water, to which she obliged, pouring him a glass from a jar kept near the bed. After the strenuous effort at the remembrance of the past, Chandran lay back exhausted. It was like the calm after a storm, for him as well as her. In a few minutes, he slipped into a deep sleep, while she kept watch over him. She must also have dozed off, as she woke when the helper came back with the medicines. Chandran's daughter also returned soon after. Shalini went to the kitchen area to lend her some help in preparing dinner. Her son came to fetch her and her father soon after and they left after their dinner, going back to her son's rented apartment.

The next few days were taken up with the preparations for the imminent wedding. Though it was to be a civil registered marriage, Shalini wanted to present her son's bride with a simple diamond set as jewellery, along with a bridal sari. She had even brought a small '*thali*' (*mangal sutra*) on a thin gold chain that Vijay was supposed to tie around the bride's neck during the marriage, as instructed by the bride's father. She had not brought any other gold ornaments with her. Her son had issued a warning, "Dear Mom, do not bring any of your heavy gold ornaments to Delhi. It is popularly held that if you wear a heavy gold 'necklace' and walk about in Delhi, you are likely to become 'neck-less' in no time. Such is the condition of the gold robbers and thieves here. Many of the robbers here even know that Malayali women are fond of flaunting their gold jewels. There have been so many incidents of gold chain snatching at gun point."

Shalini had gotten so scared on hearing this that she decided not to bring any of her jewellery from home. However, she wanted to present her would be daughter-in-law with a diamond set of jewels at least, which she could wear without fear. In this way, the chain snatchers would at least temporarily be fooled into thinking that it is artificial jewellery. Her son was willing to oblige this wish of his mother.

They went shopping over the next two days in the evenings. Her father would have a light dinner and go to bed quite early, and they went out after this. The first visit was to the diamond shop. After taking her time to select one, Shalini chose an exquisite piece, which her son approved of too. Though a bit expensive, she knew that Bhavana would love it. When her son insisted that Shalini also buy something for herself, she chose a small pendant. When she expressed her doubt about the cost, her son assured her that he had saved some money for such expenses. Now, since the wedding expenditure was comparatively lower, he did not mind his mother indulging thus.

The next day, they went to a famous textile shop. Her son had already informed her that she should restrict herself to buying only one sari, as Bhavana's usual dress was the churidar. So, she went searching for the one perfect sari which the bride could wear on the wedding day. It took her a pretty long time, but finally, she selected a light, wine-coloured silk sari, embroidered with some zari on the border. Vijay had cautioned her not to choose gaudy colours and designs, as he had seen Bhavana only in pastel shades, whenever she chose to wear saris. Shalini complied with his request, even though she personally preferred a dark shade for the bridal dress. She had brought one from home, but it was of a light, off-white colour with a zari border, for her own use. She was tired after the shopping spree. Vijay took her to a wayside South Indian restaurant, where she had some juice and her favourite 'masala dosa'.

She looked around as she ate. The restaurant looked vaguely familiar. Suddenly, she remembered that it was the same restaurant that she and Chandran used to frequent a long time ago, when they went on their long walks. How could she admit to her son that these streets were quite familiar to her? He continued to point out to her, "Mom, see that wall over there? Beyond that wall is the Delhi University. You must have come here when you stayed at campus. Bhavana's father's Kathakali Institute is also nearby. Though the management has changed hands now, since he went down with the stroke."

For some moments, Shalini was lost in the thoughts of those long lost 'campus days'. That was the time that when she had been a 'free bird', strutting about within the campus and beyond, with no responsibility except to concentrate on her studies. From there, her life had taken so many twists and turns, so much of sorrow and happiness she had come to know. Looking back, she realized that there had been bitter lessons she learnt in life. At the same time, academically, it had been the most successful time for her. On the whole, coming down to Delhi once more, meeting Chandran, talking to him, opening the door to the incidents from the past, coming to the very same place to eat by chance that they used to frequent all those years ago, the nearness to the beloved campus; all these provided Shalini with a nostalgic trip down the lane of past memories.

Chapter 21
The Finale

The rest of the events till after Vijay and Bhavana's wedding went as per schedule. The civil marriage was registered first. Only the most wanted took part in the celebrations later, Vijay's uncles and their families, and Bhavana's aunties with their immediate families. Bhavana looked stunning in her bridal attire presented by Shalini, along with the diamond set that adorned her. It looked simple, but elegant, thought Shalini. After the tying of the 'mangal sutra' and the exchanging of the rings, they were made to wear garlands of flowers, each person throwing it around the neck of the other, all this for the benefit of the onlookers, the small crowd that had gathered there as witnesses. The bridegroom looked his best in a north Indian dress. They had to sign, and thus register, in the marriage register after this. The relatives left soon after the wedding feast which was arranged at a nearby hotel. The parents and the grand–father returned to the flat. A few of their colleagues from work attended the civil wedding too.

Bhavana took a tearful leave of her father, who looked beseechingly at Shalini once more. Shalini then came back to Vijay's place. Of course, Bhavana could visit her father from time to time. She easily took over the control of the house. Shalini stayed at Delhi with her father for a few more days, helping Bhavana to settle down. They returned back to Kerala after almost a week, by flight.

She needed to take extra care of her father for a few days, as the journey had exhausted him. When alone, after returning from work and completing her work at home, she pondered and reflected over her meeting with Chandran. Where had the earlier fire, enthusiasm and energy all gone when they came face to face? She was sure that he must have dreaded the thought of meeting her after all those years. While she had also suffered some misgivings, the sight of him, broken in body and spirit, begging her to be kind to his daughter, dissolved the anger she had had for him, one that she had nursed for so many years in her mind. The doting love he had for his daughter overrode all other feelings he might have had for others, including Shalini. Though, in calling her 'Shalu', he did betray the hangover of his buried feelings for her. Perhaps, in another rebirth, as Hindus believed, they would both come together fruitfully once again. In this life, however, they were not fated to be together. Shalini let out a huge sigh and mentally closed the chapter one more time. The meeting with him had finally led to the closure, and her mind became free to move on from the past and concentrate on her present life.

A few months later, her father, now eighty-seven, had a severe attack of asthma. It worsened quickly. Her son and daughter-in-law came down to help her out. Her father had to be admitted into a nearby hospital. The attack soon took a critical turn as his lungs had also become infected. Despite good medication, his body did not respond and he finally succumbed to his illness. His age was also a negative factor. He passed away on the hospital bed. Both Shalini and her son were near his deathbed when he died. Her brother and wife had also come down. All of them left after the death rites. Shalini was now totally alone. She had almost two years of service left before retirement. Though her son offered for her to go with him, she decided to stay there for another two or three years.

She employed an older lady as a full-time servant, who helped her out around the house and was also a companion to her during her long lonely hours.

Two years sped by in a trice. She retired from her college service. Whatever property she had inherited from her husband, she sold off. The house had been kept in her husband's name, which her son now inherited. She lived a relaxed retired life. Meanwhile, her son had been sent by his office to the U.S. for two years, just as he had predicted earlier. He had taken his wife with him, who had to resign from her job in India. They had given up the rented flat and had moved their valuables to Chandran's house before leaving for the U.S.

Her son called her up regularly every other day. He seemed concerned about her living alone in the house, back in their hometown. He kept urging her to shift to a flat with day and night security and other conveniences. The present house could be given on rent. Shalini, due to her conventional nature, hated these modern flats. She felt congested when ever she went to visit some of her friends who lived in flats. The space she enjoyed in a single home, she felt she would miss in a flat. Yet, she was afraid at times to spend the night in her big home, despite the full-time servant. Thus, security was the main concern. They had heard so many stories of single women and men being attacked when staying alone, in different parts of the city. This must have been the reason that her son insisted that she shift to a flat, a spacious one, if she so preferred.

Finally, Shalini gave in to her son's demands. There was some money they had got from the sale of his father's property. She invested her portion of the money in a good spacious flat and soon moved into it. After moving into her new apartment on the ninth floor, she found that it was not as bad at all as she had imagined it to be. Since she had retired, she did not have to go out regularly. She made friends with some other inmates, whom she could meet often. She gave out her former house on rent to a good party. It was an extra income for her, besides her pension. Her son was relieved too, as he was sure that there were enough security and conveniences provided at the apartment complex. He believed his mother was safe for the time being.

She had been going to a private parallel college for a part time job, since the retirement. This was to counter her sense of loneliness after her retirement, as she had no companion at home. Since her full-time servant had left, she had begun to find it difficult to manage both her new job as well as home. Thus, she left the job soon after she shifted into the flat. This gave her more time to pursue her hobbies like reading, writing and painting, which she indulged in freely.

About a year had passed since her son had gone to the U.S. Suddenly one day, she was informed by him that his father-in-law's health had taken a turn for the worse. Both he and his wife were coming down to Delhi on urgent leave to attend to him. He told her that it would be good if she could make it to Delhi too while they were there, as he might not get enough time to visit her at their hometown. Shalini agreed and flew to Delhi. She was received at the airport by Chandran's nephew. Both he and his wife were on duty at the hospital where Chandran was admitted. She went straight to Chandran's house, had a change of clothes and some food, and then proceeded straight to the hospital. She relieved her daughter-in-law of the duty. She offered to stay back while Bhavana could go home, have a bath and come back. Her son also left for some time to have food at the hospital canteen and buy the medicines that the doctor had prescribed. She was left alone near Chandran, who was lying in the ICU. He was having difficulty in breathing. He seemed in deep sleep. She was informed that he was under sedation. Shalini waited outside the ICU.

Her mind was bringing up confusing images and thoughts. How she always seemed to be near Chandran whenever he was in a critical state like this! She had never attended to her husband like this, as his life had been over in just a few seconds, and so unexpectedly too. She had not had the time then to think thus, unlike the present moment. The more she thought about the shared incidents in their lives, the more she forgave Chandran for having betrayed her trust in him. He must have been so forced by circumstances that he did what he did to her, she thought. When he had mentioned that his relations with his wife were merely 'obligatory', he must have meant that it did not include the passion and intimacy that both of them had experienced in their relationship. It was also true that the extremes of the emotions of love and hate that she had felt for Chandran, were missing in her own married relations with her husband. Though she had consciously brushed aside all thoughts of Chandran when she became intimate with her husband and therefore was able to enjoy her relations with him, her feelings for Chandran must have gotten buried deep inside her. Now they seemed to be surfacing slowly. At the heart-breaking plight of him lying helpless on the hospital bed, Shalini felt that it was her duty to attend to him. Her daughter-in-law wondered how her mother-in-law could care for her father so selflessly. She felt lucky that she was blessed with such a wonderful mother-in-law and such a concerned husband. She would have found it difficult to manage alone without their help, she realised.

Shalini broke out of her thoughts. She was called into the ICU as Chandran had regained consciousness. She was allowed to go near him alone. He was back from some drug induced deep sleep. He recognised Shalini when she went and sat near him. She had to bend down, as he was talking in a very soft voice. She heard him say, "Dear Shalu, I am so glad you are here. I think I have come to the end of my days. What better luck than to have the woman of my dreams attending on me in these final moments? I cannot express how overwhelmed I am at this. I did not dare think that you would come here on hearing of my illness. I am so grateful. You were and always will be the love of my life."

"Hush, Chandru. How could I keep away, knowing that you or your daughter may need my help? My conscience would not have allowed me this. I forgive you for all those incidents in the past. My mind is less tense when I think of all that now."

"Oh, I am so relieved. My mind is at peace now. I had suffered such agonies thinking of how you must have felt. Even in our last meeting, you were a bit cold and distant, I felt at times."

"We did what we did due to the pressing needs of those times. Even my marriage was on the rebound. Though, in time I came to truly love and respect my husband."

"He was a lucky man, Shalu. I envy his good fortune in having married you, and to have settled down in a satisfactory relationship with you. Your son is such a great fellow. You should truly be proud of him."

"He has inherited some of the sterling qualities of his father."

"I thank you, once more, from the bottom of my heart that you came to see me in this condition. I know I look like a wretched replica of my former self. But in spirit, as far as you are concerned, I am the same Chandru, loving you with all my capacity. I can go now with the confidence that you will take care of my daughter as your own. Perhaps, with God's grace, we might be permitted to unite in another birth."

That was a speech long enough for the ailing Chandran. He had been holding her hands daintily with his own healthy hand. Now, she felt him loosen the feeble grip, as he lay back exhausted. His eyes were now closed; the effort had drained some strength out of him. She sat beside him in deep silence. What a waste of effort their love for each other had been. Like he had said just then, perhaps it would take a rebirth, another life, for the mutual love to come to fruition. It would never ever be in this lifetime.

As she gathered her thoughts, she felt tears clouding her vision. She waited for her son to come back. He came back after some time with the much-needed medicines, and some food for her from the canteen. She refused the food and said that she would have some back at Chandran's house when she went back. Once Chandran was settled and lay back preparing for a restful night, she decided to go back. Both of them mutely took leave of each other. She went back with the nephew, back to the house where Chandran had lived all these years.

Chandran's house was just as she had imagined, now that she could observe it more closely. It was very artistically decorated. There were, on the walls of the living room, two huge paintings of Chandran's earlier '*veshams*'(roles) in Kathakali attire. Her mind went back to the earlier days of their infatuation with each other. How life-like these paintings looked, hanging on the walls. She remembered once more, the incident when she had run backstage to congratulate him on his performance and he had waved her off in a distant manner. How she had suffered then. She should have known then that he would not find it difficult to keep her out of his life when the need arose. And yet, he had claimed that it was out of sheer expediency. His marriage to his cousin had been due to his mother's and uncle's pressure, he had explained, never because he wanted it in his heart. She had decided not to wait on the side lines and got married to a man of her parents' choice. Leaving Delhi and returning to her hometown was a clean break that she had consciously taken. She was lucky in her marriage and she had no regrets on that front. Yet, looking back now, she often found herself sighing for what might have been, for 'the road not taken' (Robert Frost). If only both she and Chandran could have gone ahead with their life together, following their dreams, before the tragedy struck. Once separated, they got into different marriages. She knew it was only a yearning for the unattainable, it was a futile longing. Their society would never have permitted it then, and how could they have indulged in casual friendship even now, when they were both ageing parents themselves. They were left with nothing, but to live out their desired life vicariously, through their children. Perhaps in a more liberal western society, they might have been permitted to take up their friendship once again. But in the Indian society, specially within her rigid community, she realised that even in her present times, their relationship would have to take a silent burial (along with their physical burial that signified their end of life), or risk scandal and ostracism. It was the ultimate annihilation of their lost dreams.

She came back from her reveries with a start when the servant came to serve dinner. She had an early dinner, followed by a stressful, fitful sleep, laced with nightmares. Early next morning, there was a phone call from the hospital. It was her son who informed her that Chandran had peacefully passed away in the wee hours of the morning. The previous night, he had slipped into a mild coma and had to be force fed. About midnight, he suffered some breathing problems, but the artificial intake of oxygen had calmed his breathing and he seemed to have slipped into a deep sleep. He never woke up, nor did he talk to his daughter or son-in-law at all. Shalini realised that the last person he talked to, was herself. He must have died with his heart becalmed, relieved and full of gratitude, knowing that she was there to take care of everything after he was gone. She was glad to have been of service to him thus in his last moments.

Her son also informed that the body would be brought down to Chandran's house, laid in state till afternoon, and then be taken for cremation at an electric crematorium nearby. Everything happened without a hitch. She wondered at the irony that made such a famous man, who had conquered stages with his histrionic art of Kathakali, to be taken to his grave in such a pathetic state, after an incapacitating illness. He had stopped performing actively on stage for some years now, acting merely an oral instructor. After the essential period of mourning and the last rites, her son saw her off at the airport. Both her son and wife planned to lock up Chandran's house for the time being, and took a flight back to the U.S. the very next day. Chandran's sister and son had already moved out.

Shalini arrived back at her flat at the scheduled time. She soon immersed into her day-to-day activities. For how long could she continue this, she wondered. Both the men in her life who had influenced her so strongly had bid goodbye to their lives. At one point in time, every person had to continue alone, she realised. One has to make the best of one's life, whatever the given situation. Her present was real, tangible. Her future was uncertain. Would she slip into forgetfulness herself at some point in her future? She had to make the journey to the end by herself, after successfully completing whatever duties she had left towards her children.

Meanwhile, she could mentally prepare herself for the end by indulging in religious and spiritual activities, in becoming philanthropic, thus generally making herself useful to the needy. She would indulge in her childhood passion for painting and writing with a renewed vigour, she decided. She needn't fear anyone's censure now. She was beyond caring for society's dictates. She would live her life only for herself, henceforth. She wanted to live the rest of her life without unduly depending on anyone or becoming a burden to anyone, including her son and his wife; she prayed that she would remain reasonably healthy till the very end.

Her son had taken such a liking to life in the U.S. that she had no hope for him to ever return. Now that her father was no more, her daughter-in-law would not be too interested in coming back either. If they had children, surely the kids would prefer to stay back in the U.S. Shalini knew of so many inmates from the flats nearby who had children who worked and lived in far-of places outside India. Their loneliness in having to stay away from their busy kids was only too obvious at times. The children came down to meet them on occasional visits. Shalini sensed the essential insecurity in their lives, when separated so from their offspring. And yet, they made the best use of their time, not overtly giving-in to depression or grief, keeping themselves busy, cultivating an optimistic view of life.

Her son had invited her to go with him to the States many times. He was worried that she was staying there alone. She could only politely refuse, however. She promised him that whenever he would be in need of her services, for instance when he chose to have a kid, she would surely fly to him to assist them in taking care of the child for a few years, but she had no wish to stay with him in the U.S. on a permanent basis. She loved the country of her birth too much for that. She could never think of leaving India, even Kerala, for all the conveniences of the west. When her time came, she wished to die and be buried in her homeland quietly. She would be lucky if she could possibly have her son nearby when she took her final breath, and wished like Keats, the famous English poet, to 'cease upon' the world silently and with no perceptible pain, ending her eventful life.